"This is the U.S.S. *Enterprise*, Captain James Kirk commanding. Please identify yourself."

"This is the Klingon Star Cruiser *Destructor*, commanded by Captain Kolvor. I demand an immediate explanation for this outrage."

What is the danger?
What will be the outcome?
To find the surprising answer,
read . . .

TREK TO MADWORLD

Bantam Star Trek titles
Ask your bookseller for the books you have missed

Star Trek Fotonovels™

TREK
TO
MADWORLD

A Star Trek™ Novel

BY STEPHEN GOLDIN

Introduction by
David Gerrold

TREK TO MADWORLD

A Bantam Book published under exclusive license from
Paramount Pictures Corporation, the trademark owner

Bantam edition / January 1979
2nd printing .... September 1980

ISBN 0-553-14550-9

Published simultaneously in the United States and Canada

Bantam Books are published by Bantam Books, Inc. Its trademark, consisting of the words "Bantam Books" and the por-
trayal of a bantam, is Registered in U.S. Patent and Trademark
Office and in other countries. Marca Registrada. Bantam
Books, Inc., 666 Fifth Avenue, New York, New York 10103.

PRINTED IN THE UNITED STATES OF AMERICA

11 10 9 8 7 6 5 4 3 2

dedicated to

Doña Kerns
Sally Fink
Pamela Faint

*three of the nicest
ladies one could meet at a
Star Trek convention*

AN INTRODUCTION

It is time to reveal the truth about the man most of us know as Stephen Goldin.

For many years strange rumors and furtively whispered stories have been circulating throughout the science fiction community, creating a mystique about the man, an aura of dark mystery that has been made an object of fevered speculation; but it is time to rip aside the cloak of ignorance that has fed this evil gossip and reveal Stephen Goldin as he really is. From this moment on, let the awful truth be known . . .

Stephen Goldin is a were-koala.

Whenever there is a full moon, a strange and terrifying transformation comes over him. He breaks out in a cold sweat; he starts grunting incoherently as if in pain; he rolls around on the floor, writhing in a terrible out-of-control frenzy, almost sexual in nature, all the while making the most god-awful unearthly gutteral cries. Slowly, his flesh thickens and becomes soft leathery hide. He begins to change shape, growing ever rounder and pudgier. A fine coat of gray fur sprouts all over his body, lengthening even as you watch. His nose and mouth expand, swelling into a muzzle; his ears grow large and round; his eyes turn into shiny black shoe-button orbs. A short fluffy tail sprouts from the end of his spine, sometimes even bursting through his trousers. Soon, the rest of his clothing splits apart in shreds—he develops prehensile claws and rips the last of it from him. Finally, with one last heart-rending scream, he drops to all fours and looks up at you with the most plaintive wistful expression possible—he has become positively cute! He crouches naked and revealed for the whole world to see—a chubby little marsupial!

Then, uttering weird cries of joy, he races from the house and climbs the nearest eucalyptus tree (there is one in the front yard, but it has already been stripped bare) and begins frantically munching on its leaves.

This is no mere momentary spasm of irrationality. Nay, this is part of a much larger and deliberate pattern of action. Even in his day-to-day life, Goldin practices a Koala lifestyle. Often, he can be heard about how he hates Qantas Airlines. He plans pilgrimages to Australia and keeps a scrapbook of the making strange little whimpery sounds in his throat Koala Pride Parade in Woomera. He hobnobs with three-toed sloths.

It is not for us to judge this otherwise loathsome and foul behavior. It is not for us to condemn—but imagine the embarrassment of his poor wife, the lovely and talented Kathleen Sky-Goldin (author of *Vulcan!*, a recently published Bantam Books STAR TREK novel), when she has to go down to the animal shelter and claim him the following morning.

Those of us who know and love this man, this round little furry person, have been forced by cruel circumstance to deal with this peculiar aberration. We've tried—Lord knows how we've tried—to find a way to help him sublimate this terrible urge into some socially acceptable behavior. We've even gotten him a part-time job down at the San Diego Zoo as a koala-impersonator. (Look closely on your next visit. He's the one in the glasses.) But even our most generous and helpful efforts have been to little avail. Goldin persists.

Perhaps you think I joke, perhaps you think I make light of Goldin's condition, a condition which many would regard only as a mere idiosyncrasy, or at worst, a handicap. But let me assure you, it is much worse than that. The words compulsion and obsession spring to mind. Perhaps even the words deviate and degenerate are appropriate here. Perhaps even stronger epithets might be applicable.

But does Stephen Goldin feel shame? Does he realize how disgraceful his actions are? Does he even begin to comprehend the pain and suffering and sorrow he brings to his loved ones by his constant and maddening eucalyptus munching?

The answer is no, absolutely not. Goldin is shameless. He refuses to behave by the rules of normal folk. He insists that he will not be a closet koala. He has come out into the open and declared it proudly that he *likes* being a koala. He *loves* being a koala. It may bring shudders to your heart to picture Goldin in his little gray koala suit with the bunny-foot slippers and the big round ears and the fuzzy little mittens. Think of the disgust and nausea it brings to those of us who have to bear the actual sight of him flaunting this behavior. THIS MAN BRAGS ABOUT BEING A KOALA!

Why?—you ask. Why would any normal healthy American male with a good wife and a terrific career as a well-know writer of heavyweight science fiction choose to be a koala and actively seek out the koala way of life?

It beats the hell out of me too.

Goldin claims that it's sexy. Yes, he really does. I myself have no personal knowledge of the koala life, nor do I wish to know anything more about it. Proximity to Goldin has already taught me more about koalas than any normal individual could want to know. Only my strong constitution and the dedication of long standing friendship have enabled me to control the buoyancy of my gorge. I am told that many of those who follow the koala persuasion can lead otherwise normal healthy lives, but even though some of my best friends are marsupials, it is a fact of which I remain personally unconvinced.

I suspect that the real truth behind Goldin's nauseating condition is that he has become mentally and physically addicted to this way of life. To a koala bear, the leaves of the eucalyptus—if properly aged—are a euphoriant. Why do you think the nasty little buggers are always smiling? They're stoned out of their minds!

It's that simple. To Stephen Goldin being a koala bear is a wild-eyed release from the shabbiness, poverty and moral bankruptcy of his human identity. Perhaps we could excuse the foulness of his present condition by blaming the pressures of society, or even the oppressiveness of his stunted childhood. I will not repeat the lies in his "official" biography, the ones about the kindly woodcutter and his blind sheepdog who took Goldin in when they found him still wrapped in swaddling in a basket on the doorstep of the crude little cottage they called home, and how they raised him to be a fine upstanding citizen of their small Alpine community, and how he repaid this trust by selling the cottage and putting the old coot away in a nursing home. Nay, the truth must be told; but even the truth does not excuse Goldin. We cannot blame the gypsies who stole him as a child and sold him into white slavery to a tribe of depraved outback aborigines. Yes, it's possible that this may have had some dreadful effect on Goldin's crucial formative years, but whatever responsibility there is for Goldin's foul habits must lie solely on the shoulders of Stephen Goldin himself. He is a koala of his own free will, may God have mercy on his soul.

I may be called a fuzzy thinking liberal for saying this, but it must be said, Dear Reader. I ask for a measure of understanding for this man—even an attempt at acceptance.

He does not beg, hat in hand, for your sympathy or your pity—for Goldin does not consider his condition to be a disgraceful sickness. To him it is merely an alternate lifestyle. So I ask only that you open your hearts and your minds and try to understand that there are other kinds of sanity that exist at right angles to our own, and no less valid for that difference. I ask humbly, if not for your acceptance, then at least for your tolerance. What would it hurt if the world were to make just a little more room for a lowly koala bear?

After all, even nasty little marsupials have feelings. They even have rights, loathe as decent folk may be to admit that.

And isn't that justification enough for a meager shred of your compassion?

Look—I admit, I was tempted to play on your mercies here. I could have told you that this—this disgusting perversion of Goldin's was merely an eccentricity and ask you to excuse it on the grounds that it is a necessary behavioral outlet for the man; it allows him to maintain some semblance of rationality while turning out such mind-dazzling works as *Scavenger Hunt, Finish Line, Caravan, Herds, Imperial Stars* (with the late great E.E. "Doc" Smith), and the recent highly acclaimed *Mindflight.* Yes, I suppose I could have justified his shameful life by citing some of his glorious accomplishments as validation.

Or I could have told you how Stephen Goldin has saved my life on more than one occasion, how he has always been a loyal compadre ready to offer a helping hand at a moment's notice, day or night (except those nights when the eucalyptus is especially fragrant) and used that to excuse his repulsive actions.

Or I could have even told you how Stephen Goldin once told off the warlock of West Covina and dared him to do his worst and that this bizarre koala fetish is the dastardly result of that vengeful wizard, a curse that will haunt the Goldin clan for a thousand generations. (And you think Lawrence Talbot had it rough! !)

But no—all of those things would have been hypocrisy to Goldin. Stephen Goldin is a koala bear. He has always been a koala bear. He will always be a koala bear. He refuses to hide the truth of his own life, no matter how distasteful or repellent. There is no falsity about Stephen Goldin.

Now, there may be those out there in the real world who will be offended by this revelation and the shamelessness of it, individuals who will use it as an excuse to point their fingers at Stephen Goldin and holler, "Shame! Shame!" But those who fall prey to such bigotry and ignorance will be the real losers for they will be denying themselves the pleasure of knowing one of the nicest deviated-koala-perverts you could ever hope to meet.

And they will also be daring the wrath of Goldin's newly formed militant activist group—THE MARSUPIAL LIBERATION MOVEMENT—Koala Lib!

Yes, it's here. And they are already making their demands known: Equal rights for all marsupials! (Except maybe wombats—they're *really* disgusting.) Equal opportunities for housing and employment! Protection from arbitrary discrimination! Affirmative action programs in education and industry! And guarantees that eucalyptus leaves will be covered by the food stamp program!

There it is, kids. Those are the issues.

If we aren't willing to meet these issues now, if we aren't willing to discuss them calmly as rational individuals, then we will have only ourselves to blame when our cities are once again plunged into violence and our streets are filled with shouting and angry koala bears.

You have been warned. The choice is up to you.

—David Gerrold
Sydney, Australia, 1978

1

Captain's Log, Stardate 6188.4:

We are preparing to leave orbit around Babel as soon as we pick up a pair of passengers: Kostas Spyroukis, the renowned planetary explorer who is personally responsible for locating more than thirty colonizable worlds; and his daughter Metika. The *Enterprise* has been assigned to transport them both back to their home on the colony planet Epsilon Delta 4 after their stay here and their unsuccessful attempt to have their world's status changed from colony to full member of the Federation. This is one assignment I am eagerly awaiting. Ever since I was a boy I enjoyed reading about Spyroukis's daring exploits—and the chance to finally meet him has made me feel like a cadet again.

Captain James Kirk made certain that he was in the Transporter Room along with First Officer Spock and Dr. McCoy when Captain Spyroukis materialized. This was the man who'd had so many stories and legends told about him—and Kirk had read them all, many times, as a boy. The tales of Spyroukis's exploits had been one factor in his decision to seek a career in the space services. Even now, when Kirk's own adventures had more than surpassed those of his idol, he could not help but feel slightly nervous as he prepared to meet his boyhood hero.

But the occasion proved to be a great disappointment. The man who materialized was not a demigod, but a human being like himself. Kostas Spyroukis was a short, wiry man with dark hair and a deeply tanned skin. His face was lined from years of survival under the harshest of conditions; though he was not an old man by contemporary standards, the leathery look of his skin made him seem older than he was.

Moving slowly, Captain Spyroukis stepped down from the transporter platform and glanced around the room. "You must be Captain Kirk," he said as he spotted the ship's commander. "I've heard a great deal about you. I'm honored."

Kirk blushed. He had not expected such praise from the man whom he himself worshiped. "The honor is mine, sir." Then, noticing that Spyroukis was the only person who had appeared, he added, "I thought your daughter was supposed to be coming along, too."

"She is." There was a weariness in Spyroukis's voice that seemed oddly out of place. "She just had to stop to have one last argument. Even though we lost the Council debate, she's a very headstrong girl."

As Spyroukis moved forward, Kirk could see that something was indeed wrong. The older man was moving with a slowness that bespoke some great infirmity. On Kirk's left, Dr. McCoy noticed it, too, and took a step forward to help Spyroukis.

"Is there something wrong, Captain?" McCoy asked. "I'm Lieutenant Commander McCoy, ship's surgeon. If you're not feeling well, we could have a run down to Sick Bay and I'll check you out. It'll only take a few minutes."

McCoy's concern, though, only served to irritate Spyroukis. "I'm perfectly all right," the explorer snapped. "Just a little tired, is all. I fought very hard to convince the Council I was right, and it didn't work. Maybe I got a touch of indigestion along with it, I don't know. Just let me go to my cabin and lie down. I'll be fine."

"Are you sure?" Kirk asked.

Spyroukis fixed him with a pointed stare. "Captain, I was commanding spaceships while you were still in diapers. I haven't gone senile yet. I'm perfectly capable of taking care of my own body."

Feeling properly chastised, Kirk mumbled an apology and assigned Mr. Spock the task of showing Captain Spyroukis to the visitor's cabin. After the two had gone, McCoy turned to the captain. "I'm worried, Jim. Despite what he said, he did not look well."

Kirk nodded. "I know, but he seems set against a checkup in any way, shape or form. If he were a new crewman we could order him to go anyway—but medical exams are only offered to visitors by courtesy, so I can't insist he go to your office."

"Well, I can," McCoy growled. "If anything threatens the health of the crew, I've got extraordinary powers to deal with it—and for all I know, Spyroukis may have some rare and highly contagious disease. I'll look in on him again in a little while, after he's had the chance to get settled; if things are still that bad then, hero or not, I'll have his tail down in Sick Bay on the double."

"Sir." The engineer who was manning the transporter controls interrupted the conversation. "I just received word that Miss Spyroukis is ready to beam up now."

"Fine. Beam her aboard, Lieutenant." As he spoke, Kirk moved across the room to the intercom on the wall. Pressing the speaker button, he said, "Kirk to Bridge. Prepare to leave orbit, Mr. Sulu, as soon as our second guest has been beamed up. Make course for colony Epsilon Delta 4, Warp Factor 3."

Within a few seconds there was another shimmering image on the transporter platform. As it coalesced into the form of the explorer's daughter, Kirk felt his disappointment at the unrewarding meeting with Spyroukis waning.

There may have been more beautiful women than Metika Spyroukis aboard the *Enterprise* in the past, but certainly none more original. She was shorter than average, only 160 centimeters, and slender in a way that was usually described as "willowy." Her complexion was clear and her face, if examined very closely, seemed slightly out of proportion: her mouth was a bit too small and her button nose made little impression on the mind, while her blue eyes seemed enormous and alert to everything around them. From reading her dossier earlier, Kirk knew that she was only twenty standard years old; her auburn hair, styled in a top-knot, accentuated her youth.

She was wearing a dress that could only be a designer original. It was a slinky fabric that clung to the contours of her body. The bottom was dark blue, rippling into lighter and lighter shades of blue as the eyes scanned higher up the dress. Around the hem, blending into the dark blue, was a pattern of purple in a design of seaweed; the neckline was trimmed in a material that looked like white foam. The total effect was one of the wearer rising out of a wave of blue seawater—and Metika Spyroukis was attractive enough to carry off the effect perfectly.

It was not for her beauty, though, that Captain Spyroukis had brought her along on this trip to Babel —nor was it merely the fact that she was his daughter. Kirk knew from her dossier that Metika Spyroukis— though young and perhaps inexperienced—had a brilliant mind and had already proved herself one of the ablest debaters and administrators on the colony of Epsilon Delta 4. The colonists had sent her and her father to plead their cause to the Council because those two individuals were the best the colony had to offer.

Stepping forward, the captain said, "Welcome aboard the *Enterprise,* Miss Spyroukis. I'm James Kirk, and I'd like to personally assure you of a pleasant journey home. If there's anything I can do to make the trip easier, don't hesitate to let me know."

"Thank you very much, Captain," Metika Spyroukis smiled.

At Kirk's side, McCoy cleared his throat noisily. The captain belatedly added, "This is our ship's surgeon, Dr. McCoy."

"Always a pleasure to make the acquaintance of so beautiful a lady," the doctor said.

Metika smiled a thank you at him, and McCoy beamed.

"Bones, weren't you just telling me there was something you wanted to check up on?"

"Well, Jim, there's no . . ."

"I wouldn't dream of taking you away from your duty. I'll help Miss Spyroukis get squared away in her cabin, and then I'll give her a tour of the *Enterprise*." *And maybe,* he added to himself, *I'll be able to find out from her a little more about what's wrong with her father.*

When James Kirk made it his business to escort a beautiful and otherwise unattached lady about his ship, the tour became a production of epic proportions. Depending upon the intelligence and interests of the woman involved, the excursion could feature detailed explanations of the *Enterprise*'s technical systems—engine, power plants, air recycling stations and so forth—or it could merely be a stroll through some of the more pleasant recreational areas the ship's planners had designed to keep the crew from boredom on long trips.

Metika Spyroukis was a special case. She was quite familiar with standard starship operations because of her father's background; but her father had commanded only small exploratory ships during most of his career, and a heavy cruiser of the Constellation class was a different vessel entirely. Kirk decided to modify his technical tour, and began with a swing through the automated food processing units. "These machines," he explained, "can rearrange the basic protein, fat and carbohydrate compounds in our stores

and turn them into any of the thousands of pro-
gramed meals that are registered in our computer
banks. We can feed anyone from an Abalekite to a
Zycothian with food he would swear came from home,
all automatically. Our ship's doctor can keep his pa-
tients to a precise diet if it's required—and as far as
quantities go, the machines can feed a banquet of
two hundred as easily as a single meal."

Metika was indeed impressed. "My father was always telling me that the worst part of his expeditions
was the food. The machines on scout ships have a
very limited repertoire, and they're prone to break
down at the slightest opportunity. Daddy said that
once he and his crew had to live on nothing but
bloodworm stew for over a month because the food
processor refused to make anything else."

"Truly a fate worse than death," Kirk said, raising
the back of his hand in front of his eyes in mock horror.

"It was the very best bloodworm stew," Metika
smiled, "but even so . . ."

"Yes, I can imagine. I promise you that if our food
machines break down—which they have never done
yet—I'll have our engineers fix it immediately . . . or
else we'll all dine on engineer stew. Being a captain
does have its privileges."

Kirk next led his visitor through the door from the
food processing area into the ship's gymnasium. This
was a large open room twenty meters by ten in which,
at present, more than a score of crewmembers were
spending their off-duty time. Two were working on
the parallel bars, three others were lifting weights,
and a handful were conducting a class in group cal-
isthenics; the remainder were engaged in a friendly
free-form wrestling match. No one bothered to salute
the captain as he and his guest traversed the length
of the room to the door on the other side; Captain
Kirk had long ago issued a standing order that, under
normal conditions, rank was of no consequence on
Deck Eight, where the entertainment and recreation-

al facilities were concentrated. This was the primary portion of the *Enterprise* where the crew could relax; Kirk thought it would be counterproductive to remind them of duties and responsibilities in their leisure moments.

Kirk and Metika Spyroukis went up the short gangway at the far end and went into the hallway that led them to the recreation lounge next door. This room was slightly larger than the gym, although the tables and chairs set around the perimeter made it feel more closed in. There were more people here, some eating at tables with their friends, others involved in card games, but most were grouped around the holographic display area where individual crewmembers were surrounded by three-dimensional projected situations that allowed them to test their reflexes against computer-simulated events. Those were the most popular games on the ship, the modern successor to the ancient game of pinball.

"Of course," Kirk explained as he led his guest through the lounge, pausing briefly to watch the games, "like all our facilities, these are duplicated down in the secondary hull. They have a gym and a lounge, and even a swimming pool and sundeck. The upper-deck facilities are used more often, though, because they're easier for most of the crew to reach. You can always expect to find someone in here at any hour of the day."

"Daddy tells me that all he and his crews ever got to do was read or play cards. Fortunately, he enjoys both—but there are times, I think, when he would have killed for a setup like this."

"When you've got a crew of 430 people on a mission of extended duration like ours, you have to provide them with something to keep themselves entertained, or they'll be at one another's throat in under a month. There's still not as much diversion as I'd like."

Metika's eyes widened. "What more could you possibly want?"

"A soccer field," Kirk sighed wistfully. "I think

team sports help provide even more social cohesion—
but of course there isn't room aboard even a ship this
large for any decent-sized field. We have to settle for
low-gravity gymnastics and freefall polo. I do miss
the soccer, though." He beamed at Metika. "Did you
know I was the varsity's leading scorer at the academy in my senior year?"

"Not only are you handsome, you're modest, too. I
am impressed, sir. But I was under the impression that
your ship did have some areas made to simulate an
outdoor environment."

"Exactly where we're going next." The captain took
her arm and led her through the lounge into the area
which was the ship's "park." There a gravel pathway
meandered through a blue-green carpet of sponge-
grass from the planet Delestra; the shoulder-high
stalks of prism flowers swayed characteristically back
and forth as though in some nonexistent breeze, their
shimmering petals diffracting light in rainbow pat-
terns all around; a patch of small yellow humbon-
nets droned their seductive call to any wandering
insects that might come by and fertilize them; and
further off, a clump of red honorblossoms were lend-
ing their distinctively sweet scent to the park's fresh
aroma. There were even terrestrial trees and shrubs
scattered at intervals to create little pockets of privacy
within this large open space.

Directly in front of the two humans was a fountain
that sprayed water in ever-changing hues across a
central abstract sculpture that continually was changing shape, evolving from one intriguing form to the
next in slightly over a minute. Metika smiled like a
small child and ran slightly ahead, eager to take in all
the beauty of this portion of the *Enterprise*. The corner's of Kirk's own mouth curled up into a smile as
he followed after her at a more dignified pace. He
caught up with her just as she reached the point on
the pathway closest to the fountain.

She turned to face him. "I love it, all of it. Who
would believe you could put something like this in-

side a spaceship? It seems to go on forever. Why couldn't you put a soccer field here if you wanted to?"

"The size is a carefully designed optical illusion on the part of the planners. That's partly why the trees and bushes are there—to prevent you from seeing all the way across. If you could take a straight-line view in any one direction, you'd see that the park is no more than thirty-five meters long at its widest part. It's also curved around the central axis of the circular primary hull, which would make for a very strange soccer field indeed."

He once again took her hand and escorted her down the gently winding pathway through the park. "The path wanders around in here, too," he continued, "adding to the illusion that the park is bigger than it really is. There are even the recorded sounds of insects, birds and other small animals to make us feel more at ease."

"No illusion is too good for our Star Fleet personnel, is it?"

"They did go to quite a bit of trouble, didn't they? Still, no matter how beautiful it is, we always know it's an illusion." He put an arm around her waist and pulled her slightly nearer. "An illusion can be a very lonely thing unless you share it with someone."

It was the opening line to a courtship ploy, but Metika was not going to let the captain get by that easily. Pretending she hadn't heard him she quickened her pace a bit, pulling slightly ahead of him. "Does it ever cause problems?" she asked. "I mean, a place like this might make anyone homesick for his own world. I know it makes me feel a little homesick right now."

"Is Epsilon Delta 4 like this?"

Her face reddened just a little. "Slip of the tongue. I was thinking of my old home on Parthenia, where we used to live before we settled on Epsilon Delta 4. I've only lived at the colony about two years, and sometimes I catch myself still thinking that Parthenia is home. I suppose it's a natural tendency, but I've been trying to stop it. I'm dedicated to Epsilon Delta 4—God, how I hate calling it that; that's one reason why we applied for membership status, so we could have a real name instead of some catalog designation. I'm dedicated to my new home, but there are times when it doesn't seem so homey."

"I've never been there. What's it like?"

"It's mostly very hot and very dry. Seventy-seven percent of the surface area is land, and most of that is desert—or, closer to the poles, tundra. There's only one city at the moment, Oreopolis, up on a mountain-side overlooking a large red desert."

"I agree, it doesn't sound very homey. Why put a colony there at all?"

"Minerals, for one thing. Our mountains are rich with napathic salts and corbadium deposits—plus, Daddy is very pleased with the soil. He says it's in prime virgin condition, and all it would take is an initial investment in the right crops and the land could be supporting the people within half a decade. That's why Daddy was so eager to have us declared a full member world."

"I was wondering about that," Kirk said. "Normally it takes ten to twenty years before the Council will declare a planet a member rather than a colony. They like to make sure the world can stand on its own without assistance before they grant it independence."

Metika seemed prepared to renew the argument she'd already lost in the Council's chambers. "But sometimes, too, the Council can hold back the development of a world that should be brought along much faster. A colony can't really decide its own fate; the Council allocates the money, tells it how much help it will get, how many supplies it can buy, where to concentrate its efforts. The Council considers the welfare of the Federation first; the welfare of the colony itself is of secondary importance at best."

Kirk wrinkled his brow. "Are you accusing the Council of trying to hold the colony back, keep it subjugated instead of developing it properly?"

"No . . . at least, they don't do it deliberately. But because they're more concerned with the Federation as a whole, they tend to be too conservative. They'd rather play it safe and let the process take a few years longer than try something innovative and possibly expensive to develop the world faster."

A cloud passed over Kirk's features for a moment as a very unpleasant memory crossed his mind. He remembered a colony world on which he had once lived. Tarsus IV had seemed an ideal colony at one time until its food supply was attacked and almost destroyed by a mutant fungus. Kodos, the governor of the colony, had tried something "innovative" to save it—the slaughter of half the colony's population, so that the remaining food would be sufficient to keep the other half alive.

"I'm afraid I have to agree with the Council," he said aloud slowly. "There are so many things that can go wrong with a colony world that it's best to take a bit of time to make sure things are done right. The trouble with innovative procedures is that, more often than not, they don't work—whereas patience is usually rewarded. If the colony is going to succeed, then an extra few years of waiting won't make too much difference in the long run; and if it isn't going to succeed, then there's no point of rushing in and granting it independence when it'll just have to be abandoned soon anyway. There are too many legal complications."

"I might have known you'd side with the Council," Metika said. "You're a Star Fleet Officer, you have to take the part of the Establishment. But look, my father has discovered thirty worlds that have made successful colonies. You have to trust judgment like that; he knows a good world when he sees it. This is the place he chose to settle on when he retired; you don't really believe he would have picked one with any risk, do you?

"My father picked Epsilon Delta 4 as his permanent home, the world he wants to devote the rest of his life to. He has big plans for it. First, he wants to expand the mining operations so the world will get a favorable export balance to pay for its future needs; there's more than enough mineral wealth on Epsilon Delta 4 to accomplish that. But the Council, in what passes for its wisdom, decided not to expand the mining operations just yet; they said we don't have enough people to handle the facilities."

Metika gave a wry little laugh. "We don't have enough people because there isn't enough food for any more. There isn't enough food because we don't have the capital to invest in an agricultural program that would reclaim our fertile soil and start practical farming. We don't have the capital because we can't mine enough ore to buy it. And we can't mine enough ore because we don't have enough people. It's a vicious circle, Captain, and they've locked us into it."

Kirk tried to be conciliatory. "Maybe under those circumstances you should wait until the Council can pump enough funds or material into the system to break the cycle."

"But that's just our point. We could do it on our own if they'd only let us. The Council wouldn't have to spend another credit of the Federation's money. My father's reputation is impeccable; there are private parties who'd lend us billions on just my father's word to help us get started. I even showed the Council the promissory letters. But legally they can't lend money to a colony; the Federation Council is totally in charge of a colony's affairs. If we were independent, we could get the money ourselves. Everyone on Epsilon Delta 4 is proud, both of themselves and of their world. They'd like to do this on their own, not take charity from the Federation."

Captain Kirk had led Metika on the long, roundabout path through the park, but now they came to an end, facing the door that led out to the hall and the turbolift. The ship's commander resolved to end this bickering now. The Council had turned down the colony's request for independence, and the issue was dead as far as he was concerned.

"You win," he said, throwing up his hands. "I agree that Epsilon Delta 4 should be granted its independence immediately and be made a full member of the Federation. Now all we have to do is get me a seat on the Council and find a majority of other members who agree with us."

Metika looked startled for a moment, then smiled and shook her head. "I'm sorry, Captain. I didn't mean to go on so long or rehash old battles. That fight is lost for now, and taking my frustrations out on you won't do any good. Will you accept my apology?"

"When you smile and look up so sorrowfully like that, what man could resist you?" Taking her arm, he escorted her out into the hall in front of the elevator. "Just to show you there are no hard feelings, I'm going to take you to my favorite spot in the entire ship." As they stepped into the turbolift, Kirk switched on the car's computer and said, "Deck Twelve, dorsal."

The elevator car whizzed silently off along its way, taking its two occupants first horizontally along the inner corridor of Deck Eight and then dropping diagonally down the dorsal section of the ship connecting the upper primary hull to the lower secondary hull. Even as it was doing so, the elevator car that had been stationed at the destination was automatically routed along another path so that it would end up back on Deck Eight, in the spot vacated by the captain's car.

The ride came to an abrupt end and the doors whooshed open in front of them. Kirk led his guest out behind the tube down which the elevator traveled and into a small, elliptical lounge. Two rows of chairs ran back to back down the center, facing the outer walls. "Just sit down here," Kirk said, leading Metika to one chair, "and wait and watch."

As she sat, slightly puzzled, the captain walked over to the wall and adjusted a couple of controls.

Slowly the lights in the room dimmed to a point where they were barely noticeable—and then the show began. The outer walls suddenly seemed transparent, and there before them lay the Universe in all its mystery. To talk about the blackness of space was to talk in clichés—but "blackness" was indeed a pale term to describe the depths of the darkness that lay beyond the ship's hull. Within that background of nothingness were set the stars, uncounted billions of them, each glistening like an individual gem on a velvet background. The *Enterprise* was currently cruising at Warp Factor 3, a respectable yet dignified speed; the effect was to make the stars seem to crawl slowly past toward the rear of the ship—the nearer ones moving fastest and the farther ones not at all.

"It's beautiful," Metika said. "I've seen it before in pictures and from the front screens of a ship, but never where it took up almost an entire room around me before."

Kirk moved over toward the center of the room and sat down in the chair beside her. "Anyone who could see the stars like this and *not* be affected must have a hole in the bottom of his skull where his soul leaked out. This is what life, nature, the universe are all about. Is it any wonder that almost every race has an age-old dream to travel out here among the stars and be a part of heaven?"

"My father told me there used to be a term used by divers who explored under the oceans—'rapture of the deep.' It's the same thing here, only the deep goes on forever."

The two sat quietly side by side for several minutes, admiring the beauty of interstellar space. Finally Kirk broke the long silence. "I would be honored, Metika, if you would join me in my cabin for supper tonight."

"That sounds like the opportunity of a lifetime; what woman could resist? You'll have to promise me, though—no bloodworm stew."

The captain smiled. "Now I'll have to rearrange the entire menu I'd planned. What would you say to hors d'oeuvres of Fimaldian mushrooms stuffed with bleu cheese, a sea-dollop salad coated with a thick dressing of my own creation (and heavily laced with Saurian brandy vinegar), sautéed breast of eldarine with baby peas and liyaka au gratin—and for dessert, a whipped strawberry mousse? I admit it lacks the ... *fascination* of bloodworm stew. . . ."

"Captain, you top wonder upon wonder. To find that a man with the reputation as being the finest commander in the fleet should also be an epicure of such taste. . . ."

She was interrupted by the whistling of the intercom demanding the captain's attention. Annoyed, Kirk stood up and went back to the wall control unit. Without bothering to turn off the starfield, he activated the speaker. "Kirk here."

"Sorry to disturb you, Captain," came the voice of Lieutenant Uhura, the ship's communications officer, "but Dr. McCoy seems to think it's urgent. He requests that you join him in Sick Bay immediately."

"What's the problem, Lieutenant?"

"It's Captain Spyroukis. His illness took a turn for the worse, and Dr. McCoy thinks he may be dying."

Even across the room, Kirk could sense Metika's body tensing at the news. "Tell Dr. McCoy we'll be there immediately," the captain said. "Kirk out."

2

As Kirk and Metika rode their turbolift car in silence
to Deck Seven, the captain reflected that he had spent
entirely too much time in Sick Bay since his assignment to the *Enterprise*—both as a concerned observer
and, somtimes, as a patient. *Whenever anything di-
sastrous is about to happen,* he thought, *it usually begins with a call from McCoy asking me to come to
the Sick Bay. Maybe if I just shut that section down
completely, nothing bad would ever happen again.*

As the turbolift doors swished open, Kirk took long,
quick strides toward the entrance of the main ward
where McCoy would most likely be tending his patient. Behind him, Metika almost had to run to match
his pace. There was a desperate quality to her man-
nerisms; Kirk could tell that she loved her father very
much.

The ward looked deserted at first glance, but before
the captain had more than a second to wonder where
his chief medical officer was, Head Nurse Christine
Chapel entered and told him that she and McCoy
had taken Spyroukis to the Intensive Care Unit. Impatiently, Kirk and Metika rushed through the im-
maculate corridors, fearing the worst.

Even as they approached the ward, they could see
Spyroukis through the opened door. The famed explor-

16

er was lying on an examing table clad only in a thin white sheet, surrounded by a force shield, a stasis generator and all the other miraculous devices of the modern medical profession. None of them seemed to be helping much; Kirk was experienced enough at reading the life function monitors above the bed to know that the man he so admired was in critical condition. There was a low throbbing noise coming from the instrument board, but it was far too irregular and far too low-pitched to indicate anything good.

Dr. McCoy stood beside the bed. There seemed to be, if that were possible, a few new wrinkles in his already craggy face—wrinkles of worry and perplexity. Kirk knew that McCoy tended to worry about even the most trivial of problems, but there was a depth to this particular expression that boded no good.

"How is he, Bones?" the captain asked as he walked through the door. "What's the matter with him?"

McCoy could only spread his hands in a gesture of defeat. "I wish I knew, Jim. I hadn't had the chance to pay him a follow-up visit. I was just finishing my daily report and, next thing I know, they're calling me down to Emergency to look at him. Whatever this is apparently hit him while he was lying on his bed; he tried to get up, knocked a few items off his nightstand, and crawled to the intercom to call for help. From the way he looks, I'd say it was a miracle he accomplished even that much—but then, from all I've heard, Captain Spyroukis was no ordinary man."

Metika was in the room too, right on Kirk's heels. She wanted to race to her father's side, but knew that the force shield and the stasis generator would make that impossible. Feeling impotent and helpless, she whirled on the doctor to vent her frustration. "*Is*, Doctor. *Is* no ordinary man. You're talking about him as though he were already dead."

McCoy's face softened and he modulated his voice into more soothing tones. "I'm sorry, Miss Spyroukis, I didn't mean to sound premature. Your father is definitely alive at this moment—but as for how long we can keep him that way . . ." His simple shrug spoke volumes.

Metika's gaze went from the doctor to the monitor and back to the motionless figure of her father. Without saying another word she moved over to stand beside the examining table as close as the equipment would allow her.

Kirk, however, was not about to let his doctor off the hook with such a simplistic diagnosis. "Don't you at least know what the matter is?" he asked. "Can't you make some kind of guess?"

"I could make guesses till the cows come home, and it still wouldn't do Spyroukis any good." The weariness in McCoy's tone indicated that he'd already been doing some serious theorizing, and had been unable to reach any solid conclusions. "The closest I can come is that it looks like some form of radiation poisoning—but it's a type I've never seen, and our computers are unable to identify it."

Kirk's first concern was the immediate hazard this might pose to his crew. "Is there any chance he was exposed to something on board?"

"I don't think so. I can't be sure, of course, but this has all the earmarks of the cumulative effects of a small dose over a long, constant interval. I was hoping Miss Spyroukis might be able to help me."

Metika looked up suddenly at the mention of her name, her reverie momentarily broken. "Me? What . . . ?"

"First," the doctor said, "I need some information. Has your father spent any extended periods of time in unusual environments?"

Metika gave a short, harsh laugh. "My father's the expert in unusual environments. He's probably visited more than any other human being alive."

"I don't mean just for the month or two it takes to scout a new planet. I'm talking about extended stays of months or even years."

Metika shook her head. "Daddy's job never gave him a chance to settle in one place for very long. The longest he's ever been anywhere that I can remember is just in the last two years since his retirement, on Epsilon Delta 4."

McCoy frowned and tapped two fingers lightly on the surface of his desk. After a moment, he continued, "One other thing, Miss Spyroukis. Would you let me take a few blood and tissue samples from you for comparison purposes?"

Metika, still dazed by her father's sudden illness, nodded absently. McCoy was able to take his samples painlessly, and the girl turned back to her father. The older man appeared to be resting comfortably, his condition unchanged. Just to look at him, he seemed to be in a deep, relaxed sleep. Only the low, irregular throbbing of the monitors broke that peaceful illusion.

McCoy called in one of his lab technicians, gave her the samples he'd taken from Metika and detailed the tests he wanted run. As the woman nodded and left, McCoy looked at Kirk and gestured with his head that he wanted to speak to the captain privately in another room. Kirk looked at Metika, who stood motionless as a statue by her father's bedside, and then followed the doctor into the office next door. Metika never noticed they had gone.

"Are you thinking what I'm thinking, Bones?" Kirk asked when the two were alone.

"That there's something about Epsilon Delta 4 that caused the problem?" When Kirk nodded, McCoy went on, "It seems the simplest conclusion. If Spyroukis picked up a prolonged exposure to anything, it would have to be there. And if he did, there's a good chance that some of it might show up in his daughter's body, too. If her tests show anything positive, we'll at least have some clue to what we're looking for."

"But what could it be?" Kirk mused. "Spyroukis is the most experienced scout the Federation has. He's located scores of planets and found thirty suitable for colonies; you'd think that he above all would know if there was anything of long-term danger on Epsilon Delta 4. And he certainly wouldn't pick that as the world where he and his daughter would settle permanently if anything was even slightly off."

"Perhaps it was something he discounted as negligible," McCoy suggested. "The history of medicine is full of incidents where two or more separate factors, each totally harmless in itself, combined under the proper circumstances to produce some pretty lethal results. I'd suggest you put Spock to work on that particular problem; if anyone can sort through the millions of insignificant facts and come to the proper conclusion, it'll be Spock and that computer brain of his."

Captain Kirk felt a light chill as the doctor spoke. For McCoy to recommend handing a problem to Spock, the situation would have to go far beyond serious—it had to be cataclysmic!

Five hours later, Kirk convened the small meeting with his two closest friends in the Deck Six Briefing Room. Seated across the large table was Dr. McCoy, looking more dour and glum than ever. To Kirk's right sat Spock, rigid yet relaxed, as though military posture were the ultimate purpose of his body's design. He had a sheaf of written notes on the table in front of him, but Kirk knew he would never look at them. In all his long acquaintance with Mr. Spock, Kirk had yet to see his first officer unprepared for a briefing; he suspected that Spock memorized all the data just before coming into the Briefing Room.

"First off," Kirk opened solemnly, "I need a status report. How is Captain Spyroukis?"

"Deteriorating slowly," McCoy answered. "I don't think we can hold him more than another hour or two at the rate he's slipping."

Kirk grimaced even though the news was not unexpected. "Any more luck on tracking down exactly what it is we're dealing with?"

"I presume you mean the tests on Miss Spyroukis.

Yes, you could say there's been some luck. She's got it, too." As the captain reacted to this, McCoy held up a hand to calm him. "Oh, not to any serious extent yet. We had to perform the tests three times just to make sure of the conclusion. The indications were so faint that there was some chance it might be minute flaws in our instruments. We've all but eliminated that possibility. Miss Spyroukis is perfectly healthy at the present, but if she's exposed to the conditions her father experienced for any long periods of time, she could develop the same symptoms."

"Any chance of treatment?"

McCoy shook his head sadly. "None that I know of. I've tried all our standard antiradiation therapies, and even a few nonstandard ones. The disease has been simmering below the surface so long, wrecking the body internally before it became apparent, that there's nothing I can do to slow its progress. I suspect Captain Spyroukis has been having symptoms for quite some time and merely shrugged them off as signs of advancing old age. Mild dizzy spells, touches of indigestion, thinning of hair, things like that. Like cancer, by the time the problem becomes really noticeable it's far too late to do anything."

The captain turned to the imperturbable Mr. Spock. "How have you done at your end? Is there anything about Epsilon Delta 4 that could be the root of the trouble?"

"I'm afraid that I, too, am limited to guesswork and speculation. The potential exists, but in the absence of extensive laboratory tests I cannot state for certain that my suppositions about the causative factors are correct."

"I'll accept your qualification, Mr. Spock," Kirk said, mildly annoyed at the Vulcan's customary circumlocution. "At the moment, though, any supposition is better than none at all, and yours have a high record of proving out. Please continue."

Spock gave the captain an almost imperceptible nod of his head. "Very well. Since the problem seemed to be a form of radiation poisoning, I looked first at the largest single source of radiation available to the Epsilon Delta 4 colony: its sun. Our ship's computer had in its information bank the original records obtained by Captain Spyroukis on his initial investigation of the planet, in addition to periodic updates made by scientists at the colony since its foundation. I performed a spectrographic analysis of that star's radiation curve and compared it to analyses that had been made previously. The results concurred. Epsilon Delta 4's sun is a strong emitter of zeton radiation."

"But zeton radiation's effects are well known," McCoy interrupted. "It doesn't cause illness like this."

If the interruption to his carefully prepared presentation in any way affected Spock, he did not show it. His tone remained level as he continued, "Quite correct, Doctor. Experiments with zeton radiation have been carried on for years, and have proven beyond any rational doubt that zeton radiation in any naturally occurring quantities is totally harmless to Terran human beings, as well as most other races in the Galaxy. It was not the zeton radiation per se that caused Captain Spyroukis's illness.

"My next thought was that there might be some other radiation to blame. Aside from the zeton radiation, the local sun's output is not vastly different from that of Earth's sun, so nothing further was to be gained there. I learned that Epsilon Delta 4 is rich in minerals and I thought that perhaps some radioactive materials near the colony's main settlement, in combination with the zeton radiation, might have produced this effect. But this supposition, too, proved wrong. There were no recorded deposits of radioactive materials within hundreds of kilometers of the main settlement; the minerals the colony wants to mine are all strictly conventional ones.

"Since radiation alone could not account for the phenomenon, I turned to the next most pervasive aspect of the colony's environment—the air. Epsilon Delta 4's atmosphere is almost identical to Earth's, but with one major exception: instead of comprising only one percent, as on Earth, the element argon comprises slightly less than two percent of the atmosphere on Epsilon Delta 4."

"But argon's an inert gas," McCoy argued. "Even in this slightly higher concentration, its mere presence in the lungs and bloodstream would scarcely matter."

"Again, Doctor," Spock said evenly, "your assumption is correct as far as it goes. I decided to take it a step further, however. There have been a few laboratory experiments reported on the effect of strong zeton radiation upon argon. It was found that argon atoms bombarded with continuous dosages of zeton radiation tended to become unstable. In some cases they became ionized, while in others they tended to lose their chemical property of inertness and could even recombine with other atoms lower on the periodic chart."

"Like hydrogen, oxygen, carbon and nitrogen," McCoy muttered.

"Precisely." If ever a Vulcan could look pleased with himself, Spock did at that instant. "The effect of this recombination in any short-term circumstance would of course be negligible, considering how small an amount of argon was available to begin with and how small a percentage of argon actually becomes unstable due to the zeton radiation. But living tissue is a very sensitive material, as you know, and the cumulative effect of this unusual reaction could well lead to the symptoms you describe."

McCoy was silent for a moment, pondering what Spock had told him. "I would never even have thought to look for something like that—but now that you point it out, it does look like the logical answer."

"Of course, Doctor," Mr. Spock said flatly.

"But there's nothing we can do to change either the sun or the atmosphere of Epsilon Delta 4," McCoy continued, half to himself. "Like Metika Spyroukis, all the other colonists on that world are being exposed to this unknown menace day in and day out. The very air around them will kill them all unless something is done—and quickly."

All three men around the table knew what that implied. Epsilon Delta 4, no matter how ideal a colony world it seemed, would have to be abandoned as a human settlement. Its cities would be dismantled, the hopes of its settlers crushed. All the people who'd been living there would have to be evacuated before they, too, were struck down by the mysterious illness that was killing Kostas Spyroukis.

And Metika Spyroukis, who had just traveled to Babel to argue the case for Epsilon Delta 4's independence, was not likely to be pleased that her newly adopted homeland would soon be deserted once more.

3

I have sent through a Priority-1 call to Star Fleet Command, outlining the situation on colony world Epsilon Delta 4 as nearly as we can estimate it. Star Fleet acknowledges receipt of our hypotheses, and promises to get their best scientific teams to work on the problem at once. They will apprise me of the situation the instant they have any results.

Meanwhile, the *Enterprise* continues on its original course to Epsilon Delta 4. I have taken the liberty of increasing our speed to Warp Factor 4; in the event Star Fleet confirms our worst fears, we will want to reach the colony in a hurry to begin the evacuation. My chief engineer is currently working on contingency plans to house the evacuees aboard the ship if and when that becomes necessary.

Metika Spyroukis has not left her father's side since he was stricken. I believe I'll have the hardest task of all—telling her that Epsilon Delta 4 may have to be abandoned.

Much to Kirk's surprise, Metika took the news about the colony far better than he had expected. Perhaps the gravity of her father's condition had made all other matters seem unimportant, for when the captain

25

took her into McCoy's private office and explained Spock's hypothesis as delicately as he could, Metika's only response was to nod slowly.

"I was afraid it might be something like this," she said. "My brain obviously isn't in gear today, or I'd have figured it out myself a lot earlier. Why else would Dr. McCoy take samples from me unless he suspected something that would be common to the people on my world? I didn't have much to do except think while standing beside my father's bed, and I've had a little time to get used to the idea."

"I have to admit, you're taking this much more calmly than I expected," Kirk said. "After the impassioned argument you gave me earlier, I was afraid you'd fight the idea of abandoning the colony."

"My father was always a realist, Captain. He had to be, to achieve as much success as he did in such a risky field. He brought me up the same way. You don't survive if you want one thing and all the facts point in the other direction. I'm disappointed, certainly. But if all the facts tell us that to stay on Epsilon Delta 4 is to die, then we must evacuate it as quickly as possible. I may only be twenty years old, Captain, but I'm not a child."

She hesitated, as though wondering whether to bare her soul still further to this relative stranger. Looking down at her feet, she continued more softly, "I wanted the colony to succeed more for my father than for myself. You don't know how much this meant to him—to have his final home be the last world he himself discovered. My father has done so much for the Federation so selflessly for so many years that we—everyone at the colony—wanted this world to succeed, as a lasting memorial." She looked back up into Kirk's face. "And now it has to be abandoned. The irony is awfully heavy."

"We're not positive yet," Kirk hastened to point out. "We may not have to . . ."

"Don't tease me with false hopes, Captain; the letdown would only be more cruel. You've explained your science officer's reasoning, and it's eminently sound. Let me make a clean emotional break and get it over with."

She's a strong-willed woman, Kirk thought admiringly. *Far older than her age.*

At this moment, McCoy opened the door and broke into the conversation. "Jim, Spyroukis has regained consciousness. I don't know how long it will last."

Metika almost sprang out of her chair. "Let me see him."

McCoy looked slightly embarrassed. "He, uh, he asked specifically to see the captain first. Alone."

Metika's face fell. "Oh. I see." She took a deep breath and straightened her shoulders. Her voice was carefully neutral as she continued, "My father was always strong on military tradition. One skipper to another, eh? I understand." Then her composure broke down completely. "Don't take too long, Captain. I'd ... I'd like to say goodbye, too."

Kirk rested a hand lightly on her shoulder for a moment and gave her a silent nod. Without another word he walked into the adjoining room where Kostas Spyroukis lay, and the door whooshed gently shut behind him.

Despite the stinging scent of antiseptics, Kirk could swear he smelled the sour-milk-and-urine odor of death in the room. The indicator marks on the monitor above the patient's bed were fluctuating up and down, but never far from zero. The throbbing of the machine was so slow that at first Kirk thought it had stopped altogether.

Kostas Spyroukis lay motionless on the table, surrounded by the faint bluish glow provided by the stasis generator. At first glance he appeared utterly lifeless, but then Kirk noticed that his eyes were slightly open and the lids were fluttering faintly. Kirk walked quietly to the edge of the force barrier. "Captain Spyroukis?"

The patient was too weak to turn his head more than a couple of centimeters, but his eyes did track in the direction of Kirk's voice. His lips moved feebly, and Kirk had to strain to hear what he said.

"Your doctor told me, Captain. I had to talk to you to . . . set certain facts right."

"Set things right?" Kirk was perplexed.

"Yes, I . . . only another captain would realize my problems. Only another captain could absolve me."

" 'Absolve?' That implies guilt. sir. and I—"

"I knew about the . . . possible danger." Although Spyroukis's voice was barely audible. there was still enough strength in the personality behind it to cut Kirk off in midsentence.

"You knew? But then why—"

"Please don't interrupt. Captain. I don't . . . have long, and each word's painful. I didn't know for certain it would do this. but I did know what zeton radiation does to argon. I . . . glossed over it in my report. I wanted that world, Captain. I wanted a place to settle and . . . raise my daughter properly. After sixty years in space, I needed roots.

"All my other worlds were too well settled. I wanted someplace where . . . where I could be a founder rather than just a discoverer." He paused for a weak cough. "Did you know. Captain, that of all the worlds I found for colonies, not one was ever named for me? Does that sound terribly vain, to want a . . . a monument? Am I just a silly old man, Captain?"

"You already have a monument," Kirk said softly. "Myself for one; reading about your exploits was one of the things that decided me on a career in space. I'm sure there are thousands of others, too. As long as the record of your exploits lives on, you'll stir young people to courage and adventure."

"It's not the same." There was a weakness in Spyroukis's voice that worried Kirk enormously. When the explorer did not speak again for almost a minute, Kirk started to turn to call for McCoy and Metika. But Spyroukis was not finished.

"When I felt myself becoming sick, I suspected even

more. I knew I'd have to act fast. I tried to rush the Council. Foolish—they never rush, but I knew I didn't have much time."

The older man, with a great effort, turned his head the rest of the way so that he was now looking directly at Kirk. His eyes were slightly glazed, but Kirk did not doubt for an instant that Spyroukis could see him clearly. "Tell me I wasn't wrong, Captain," he whispered. "Tell me I didn't condemn hundreds of good people to death merely for the sake of an old man's vanity."

"You didn't," Kirk said quickly. "We're on our way there this instant. We'll be able to evacuate them in time, I'm sure of it."

Spyroukis's body relaxed visibly. "Thank you, Captain. Whether it's true or not, it's a great comfort." He hesitated. "Metika . . ."

"Do you want her?"

"In a second. Please, Captain. Please don't ever tell her I knew. Not anyone, really, but especially not her. She . . . she thinks I'm so unflawed. . . ."

"Don't worry." Kirk wanted to reach out and lay a reassuring hand on the dying man's shoulder, but the force shield and stasis generator prevented the gesture. The best he could do was project confidence as he said, "We'll evacuate all the people in time and your daughter will never know that you suspected anything was wrong from the beginning."

Spyroukis closed his eyes for a long moment. "Thank you, Captain. Now, please send her in."

Kirk left the room feeling a heavier weight on his shoulders than there had been when he entered. With a nod of his head he indicated to Metika that it was all right to see her father now, and the young woman immediately entered the ward. As the door closed behind her, Kirk sat down wearily behind McCoy's desk. The doctor looked at him and was about to speak, but read the expression on his friend's face and chose to say nothing.

Ten minutes later, a teary-eyed Metika Spyroukis emerged from the ward and informed them both that her father was dead.

"The question we have to face now," McCoy said, "is how much time do we have for the evacuation? Why was the illness much more advanced for the father than for the daughter, and how much more exposure could she risk before she reaches the fatal dosage?"

It was now ten hours after Kostas Spyroukis's death. McCoy had performed a quick but thorough autopsy on the explorer's body and found, as expected, an overabundance of argon within the system. After that, Kirk had had the sorrowful task of presiding at the funeral of the man he'd admired so greatly. The words he found to say were, he thought, totally inadequate to express the scope of Spyroukis's achievements in space exploration; but, however clumsy it seemed to him, his service was taken well by the crewmembers in attendance and those listening to the service from their posts. Metika thanked the captain and said that her father would have been proud to hear the things Kirk had said about him.

Though bodies in space were usually disposed of by cremation within the ship's nuclear furnaces, James Kirk somehow could not envision such an end for his childhood hero. Instead, he returned to the old Terran naval tradition of sliding the flag-draped coffin out of the ship through a hatch in the shuttlecraft hanger, with a flurry of photon torpedoes exploding outside around the coffin to provide the appropriate fireworks. *It's only right*, Kirk thought, *that Kostas Spyroukis's body be returned to space, so that even in death he can continue to explore its depths as he did in life.*

Now, with that sad chore accomplished, a council had been convened in the Briefing Room. In addition to Kirk, Dr. McCoy and Mr. Spock, those seated around the large conference table were Chief Engineer Montgomery Scott, Personnel Officer Ramona Placer and passenger Metika Spyroukis. There had not, as yet, been any message received from Star Fleet to confirm or deny Spock's hypothesis, but Kirk knew that he could not wait until the orders came to start administrative procedures. A good command officer anticipated his orders and was ready to implement them the moment they were received.

Metika Spyroukis, her eyes now dried of tears, looked up at Dr. McCoy as the physician spoke. "My father's case would be the most advanced because he spent more time on the planet than anyone else. Remember, he was the explorer who discovered it, and before the Federation Council will approve a world for colonization it must be proved conducive to human habitation. My father and his crew lived there for several months before the first colonists were ever allowed to settle—myself included."

"How many months?" McCoy asked.

"I'm not precisely sure. Three to four, I think. Then he left it to return to Star Fleet and file his report. His retirement took about the same time to be processed as the planet's colonization status, and Daddy and I arrived on Epsilon Delta 4 with the first shipload of settlers six months later."

"Did any others from your father's crew settle on the planet as well?" Spock asked.

"No, he was the only one."

"Then unless his rate of reaction to the disease is atypical, we may assume that his case was three or four months further advanced than that of anyone else on the planet. Dr. McCoy's tests on Miss Spyroukis bear this assumption out; while traces of the disease do appear in her system, they are minute and, for the moment, nonlethal."

"Then we've got nearly three months in which to evacuate the colony," said the chief engineer. "That should be plenty of time."

"I'm afraid not, Scotty," Kirk said, looking to McCoy for confirmation. The doctor nodded.

"You see, Scotty," Kirk went on, "with a disease this unusual, we have no way of knowing when the lethal level was reached. Spyroukis was three months ahead of the others as far as the actual death goes— but how do we know we could have saved him if we'd learned of his condition one or even two months ago? We simply don't know when the point of no return is reached. The only thing we can do is assume the worst possible case and get every one off that planet as quickly as possible."

Kirk nodded gravely and looked again at Metika. "How many interstellar ships do the colonists have at their disposal?"

The girl answered with a wry smile. "That depends on whether we're lucky enough to have a ship in port at the moment. The answer in general is none. We're so far off the normal trade routes that a ship may only stop by once or twice a year. And as for ships of our own—well, we couldn't even afford all the mining gear we wanted; there was no way we could have afforded anything bigger than a private spaceyacht."

Kirk sighed. He'd been afraid that would be the case. Epsilon Delta 4 was located near the outer perimeter of the sector the *Enterprise* patrolled. Any other Star Fleet vessel large enough to help with the evacuation was likely to be several weeks' travel time away at best. If private cargo ships visited the planet as seldom as Metika said, then the *Enterprise* was the only ship that could make it to the colony in time.

"In that case," Kirk said aloud, "we'll have to use 'worst possible case' planning. We'll assume that no other ships are in the immediate vicinity to help with the evacuation. The question then becomes whether the *Enterprise* can take on all the colonists at once. Metika, how many people live on Epsilon Delta 4?"

"Approximately 680."

There was a silence around the table as the rest of the company digested that figure. After Kirk had given it enough time to sink in, he turned to his Chief

Engineer. "Scotty, can the ship's life support systems handle that many extra people aboard?"

Scotty was frog-eyed considering the logistical difficulties that would entail. "I dinna know, Captain," he admitted. "The ship is designed to hold 430 in comfort. Squeezin' in half again as many could be done by gettin' a mite friendlier with everyone around ye—but 680 more . . ."

"There's plenty of room," Metika spoke up. "There's lots of open area in the recreation rooms and the park that I saw yesterday. At worst, there are kilometers of corridors. If each colonist brought only a few possessions with him, there would still be plenty of space for everyone."

Scotty looked directly at her with a hard but not unsympathetic glint in his eye. "Aye, miss—and what do they eat, and what do they drink, and—when the temperature of the air around them starts risin'—what do they breathe?"

"Scotty's right, Metika," Kirk cut in hastily. "Space is the least of our problems. The ship's resources were calculated for 430, and suddenly we're talking about more than 1100—almost three time the original number. Any system can break down when you try to push it at three times normal. We have plenty of food, but distributing it will be no simple problem. The body temperatures of 1100 people crowded together will put a strain on the ship's environmental system. That many people, too, eliminate a great deal of waste products, which have to be disposed of; there's another strain on the ship. The problems aren't insurmountable, but they are large and they must be considered."

"Begging your pardon, Captain," interrupted Mr. Spock, "but the problems need not be as complex as you suggest."

"What do you mean?"

"Merely that it would not be necessary to transport 1100 people at one time. Consider: a Constellation class starship like the *Enterprise* can be run efficiently

with a skeleton crew of 57 people. That has been demonstrated on numerous occasions. I would suggest
leaving all but the minimum number of our own crew
down on the surface of Epsilon Delta 4 while we take
the colonists to safety, then come back and pick up
our crew again."

Lieutenant Placer, the personnel officer, chose this
moment to speak. "But then we'd be exposing our
own people to this menace."

"It has been shown," Spock explained patiently,
"that this 'menace' exists only when one is exposed to
it for long durations. It would certainly take us no
more than a month to transport the colonists to some
safer world and then return for our crew. During that
time, their exposure to the hazardous conditions would
be minimal. In the meantime, while the ship would
indeed be crowded during the evacuation operation,
the number of people aboard would be less than 750,
rather than 1100 as was being discussed previously."

At this moment, a message was piped down from
the Bridge. Lieutenant Uhura's voice filtered in over
the intercom: "Captain, a message from Star Fleet.
'Laboratory tests confirm your hypothesis of zeton ra-
diation/argon connection. Immediate evacuation of
Epsilon Delta 4 colony imperative. Proceed with all
possible speed and take whatever actions necessary to
save lives.' "

Kirk looked at the grim-faced people seated around
the table. The question before the house had just
ceased being academic.

4

Pursuant to orders, the *Enterprise* is on its way to evacuate the Epsilon Delta 4 colony. We have radioed ahead and explained the situation to the local officials, who received the news with understandable anger, dismay and confusion; however, when Metika Spyroukis explained further—including a detailed account of her father's death—they conceded the need for action and promised their utmost cooperation. Evacuation work at their end will begin immediately, so that they will hopefully be ready for us by the time we arrive.

Meanwhile, I have assigned Lieutenant Placer the job of deciding which crewmembers will remain behind on the planet to make more room aboard ship for the evacuees; Lieutenant Commander Scott has the task of readying the ship to carry nearly double its normal complement of people. Knowing the competence of both officers, I'm positive the *Enterprise* will be ready by the time it reaches Epsilon Delta 4.

Lieutenant Ramona Placer was one of the "forgotten" officers aboard the *Enterprise*—a fact which she chose to accept as a compliment. As personnel

officer, it was her job to see that the entire crew performed their jobs smoothly and without complaint.
If there were any complaints, it was her duty to hear
them first, and take care of them before they became
of major concern. It was very much to her credit that
ninety-eight percent of the problems she dealt with
never reached the attention of Captain Kirk except
as buried incidents in her official report—leaving the
captain's mind free to deal with the more crucial issues involved in running a starship.

Now, at the captain's orders, she was frantically
making lists. In theory, the book of emergency regulations spelled out exactly what the ship's complement
should be under skelton crew conditions; but in practice, the personnel officer actually had wide discretion
as to who should stay and who should be left behind.

For instance, regulations stated that the ship must
maintain a minimum of six gunnery officers; but it
was Placer's job to pick *which* six out of the twenty-
four currently aboard the *Enterprise*. A less conscien-
tious personnel officer might simply have picked the
six with the highest seniority and rank, or else left
the decision to the computer; to Lieutenant Placer,
such thinking represented an abrogation of her responsibility. It was her duty to make the *best* decision,
not merely the easiest.

One crewman named Solari was the highest-ranking
gunnery officer aboard, chief of the gunnery team and
a very logical choice to remain as one of the skeleton
crew; but his background information indicated that
he had been born and raised on a colony world much
like Epsilon Delta 4. The crewmembers left behind
would have to cope with primitive conditions for perhaps a month before the *Enterprise* was able to return
for them; a man experienced at living under such circumstances would be of enormous help at smoothing
some of the problems that were bound to arise.

Another crewmember, Ti-Chen, was on her first
cruise out from the Academy. Placer had assigned her
to gunnery because that was where her aptitude and

interests seemed to be strongest. Her inexperience at her post would seem to make her a strong candidate to be left behind on Epsilon Delta 4—but some instinct at the back of Placer's mind made her hold up her choice. All the indications were that Ti-Chen would make a first-class gunnery officer one day. Manning her post under emergency conditions such as these would put her in a concentrated learning situation where she would be forced to do the jobs of several people simultaneously. At the same time, since the *Enterprise* was not likely to come under battle conditions, Ti-Chen's inexperience was not likely to hurt the ship. There was a chance that the *Enterprise* could end up with a much better gunnery officer than it started out with—which Placer considered to be making the best of a bad situation.

Of course, she couldn't just put all the inexperienced gunners at the posts; there would have to be some balance. She reconsidered whether she wanted Solari to stay behind, or whether one of the other experienced gunnery officers might make just as good a teacher for Ti-Chen. . . .

Placer, of course, had put her own name on the list of those to stay on Epsilon Delta 4. Emergency regulations did not provide for a personnel officer on board under skeleton crew conditions.

Scotty and his engineering crew, meanwhile, were preparing the ship for what they thought of as an invasion. "Infestation" might even have been a more accurate, if less diplomatic, term to describe Scotty's thoughts. His engines, *his* ship, were precious to him, and the idea that soon a horde of strangers would be barging in here, trampling through the *Enterprise* and violating the integrity of its most private inner recesses, was more than slightly repellent to him. True, he recognized the necessity of what was being done; Mr. Scott was, at heart, a very kind and generous man. Under normal circumstances he would scarcely harm a fly; but let that fly buzz too near his engines and he would hunt it down with a phaser set on kill. He knew the evacuees would never deliberately damage the ship; but in their ignorance they could wreak a great deal of unintended havoc along the way. And there would be so many of them. . . .

The *Enterprise* was such a large and complicated piece of equipment that there were many interconnecting systems to be taken into account. The first thought, of course, was to oxygen regeneration; nothing else would be important if the people within the ship couldn't breathe. The *Enterprise* had its own filters and gardens where carbon dioxide was processed back into breathable oxygen; Scotty had to see to it that these processes would still function at nearly double their standard capacity. There were large pumps that kept the air circulating freely throughout the ship, and these were also tied into the environmental quality systems. Pushing them at twice their usual speed would put a greater strain on them, and could lead to premature breakdowns. Added to the problem was the fact that, with only a skeleton staff aboard, there would be fewer people to tend the machines if they *did* break down.

To forestall such eventualities, Scotty was having his crew check out every single mechanical component now, while there was still the manpower available to deal with potential problems. The entire ship was being dismantled from within, one piece at a time, and each piece was given a rigorous testing to make sure that it was in prime condition for the ordeal that was to come. If it showed the slightest sign of wear it was replaced immediately with a brand new version; or, if no replacements were at hand, the piece was listed in the computer as a potential source of trouble and plans were drawn to be able to bypass that system at a moment's notice and switch to a backup should the initial component fail under stress.

Given unlimited time and manpower, the work would have been routine, but Scotty did not have either. His engineering staff was, he'd often boasted, the finest in Star Fleet, but they were still only finite beings of limited strength and endurance. The *Enterprise* was a large ship and his team was giving him a superhuman effort, but there was only so far flesh-and-blood people could be pushed before they dropped in their tracks—or worse, before their eyes became so glazed with fatigue that they failed to spot something vital and made a crucial mistake. Despite the need for haste, Scotty vigorously enforced a mandatory rest rotation schedule so that no one became too tired to perform his job well.

He had promised the captain that he would have the ship ready by the time they reached Epsilon Delta 4. He had never broken his word to Kirk yet, and he didn't intend to start now. But it would be a race against time. . . .

Up on the Bridge, Kirk was doing his utmost to cut that time down even further. He had already ordered the ship's speed up to Warp Factor 7, which was well into its emergency range; he had even debated with himself the possibility of increasing to Warp 8, but decided against it. At such high speeds, the ship itself began to experience mechanical difficulties; the *Enterprise* had survived such speeds before, but only because it had simultaneously undergone extensive babying by Scotty and his brilliant engineering staff. Scotty now had enough on his hands without having to worry about the ship falling apart from excessive speed.

Still, even at Warp Factor 7, the computer predicted it would take the Enterprise five more days to reach Epsilon Delta 4. Kirk chafed. Five days was a long time, and he wondered how many people might be doomed to die of the mysterious argon poisoning in the meantime. Metika, too, was gripped with impatience; though she was not permitted on the Bridge, she utilized every opportunity she could find to convey her sense of urgency to the captain. There had to be something he could do to get them there faster.

In frustration, Kirk had the computer illustrate their course for him. He hoped in this way to see whether there were any shortcuts that could be taken, any edges that might be shaved to gain them an extra few minutes. He was scarcely prepared, however, for what the screen showed him, and he immediately called for Mr. Spock to add his own interpretation to the results displayed.

"Am I going prematurely senile, Mr. Spock," Kirk said, "or does the computer simulation show that we are going more than seventy lightyears out of our way?"

Spock studied the viewscreen dispassionately. "Although the two alternatives you offered are not mutually exclusive, Captain, I would have to say that the second offers the greater likelihood of truth."

In fact, their course as plotted on the viewscreen was very much the long way around. It showed the path of the *Enterprise* making a wide curve through space along its route from Babel to Epsilon Delta 4. There were no major star systems or enemy territories along the straight line route between the two end points, and yet the ship was swerving widely out of the optimum path.

"Mr. Sulu," Kirk said, "please explain why our route is taking such a large detour."

The helmsman examined the projected course on the screen. "That's the course I plotted, Captain. When we left Babel I entered the coordinates of Epsilon Delta 4 into the navigational computer, and this was the path the computer recommended." Even as he spoke, the lieutenant was punching a set of buttons on the instrument console before him. "I took it for granted that the computer would design the optimum course, but I'm checking now on why. . . . Ah, there it is. Computer shows the blank space between Babel and Epsilon Delta 4 as being a Navigational Hazard, Class Two, sir."

"Mr. Spock, check the ship's records and find out the nature of the hazard," Kirk said—but found himself talking to empty air. Mr. Spock, ever the efficient officer, had anticipated the command and had already turned to his own console to do just that.

Kirk sat calmly in his large command chair while he awaited the science officer's response, reviewing in his own mind what he knew of such things. Interstellar space was filled with all sorts of obstacles to travellers. Some, like black holes, nebulae and starswarm debris, were obvious. Others were less so; an ion storm, for instance, could sweep catastrophically from out of nowhere, wreak untold havoc on an unprotected ship, and then pass again out of existence.

When interstellar exploration had begun, there had been no way to predict some of these strange transient phenomena, and many ships had been lost to their capricious violence. Only recently had a theory on the nature and formation of ion storms begun to emerge—based in large part on the volumes of data collected by valiant exploration ships like the *Enterprise*—which made it possible to predict when and where problems might occur.

The Navigational Hazard Classification Authority had been established by Star Fleet less than twenty years ago, and already had proven itself one of the most important branches of the Service. It provided information to all interstellar vessels, both military and civilian, regarding the potentially hazardous spots along known routes. All ships' navigational computers allowed for these areas of hazard while making their computations. In the instance of the *Enterprise*'s current course, the computer had simply taken the positions given by Sulu, noted that a navigational hazard lay in the direct path, and routinely plotted a trajectory around the hazard without bothering to notify anyone of the change. There was no reason why it should notify anyone; avoiding specifically marked navigational hazards was built into its program. It would require a manual override to change that.

The fact that this was a Class Two hazard was encouraging. Class Two was reserved for permanent, nondynamic, low risk hazards; that sort of impediment was a danger largely to smaller civilian ships that did not carry the extensive shielding that the *Enterprise* did. Kirk's ship had crossed many areas of Class Two hazard with no difficulty at all when the necessity had arisen; perhaps, if they were able to cut through this one as well, they might make much better time to Epsilon Delta 4. It would all depend on the exact nature of the hazard.

Mr. Spock was ready with his report in just a few minutes. "The hazard area we are skirting appears to be a region of extreme nebulosity, Captain. The density of interstellar material is 87.6 times higher than normal."

Kirk refrained from the temptation to sigh with relief. Instead, he merely asked in a conversational tone, "Any evidence of large solid obstructions or protostellar objects within the cloud?"

"None on record, Captain. Because the Epsilon Delta 4 colony was settled so recently, not much exploration has yet been made of this immediate volume of space. The preliminary work was completed by mapping the outlines of the region of nebulosity; further studies of the interior are planned, but have not yet been carried out."

Kirk shifted position in his chair as he digested the news Spock had delivered. Interstellar space could, in general, be defined as a rarified nothingness, a more perfect vacuum than anything achievable in a laboratory. Typically that meant only twenty atoms, usually of hydrogen, to be found within one cubic meter. There were occasional clouds such as this one, however, where the density increased markedly; here, as Spock had inferred, there might be as many as 1800 atoms per cubic meter.

That does not sound like a very great amount— and it isn't in comparison to the density of typical solid matter. But when a large massive object like the *Enterprise* is traveling at Warp 7—343 times the speed of light—it enters the realm of trans-Einsteinian physics in which even minute changes can produce drastic results.

The main worry was friction. Moving at hundreds of times the speed of light, the *Enterprise* passed through untold billions of cubic meters every second—and, at those post-relativistic velocities, each atom encountered behaved as though it were many times its actual inertial mass. The factors of friction and drag, even in normal space, were far from negligible, and had been taken into account by the designers of the *Enterprise*.

Moving through the thin cloud of nebulous material, the force of friction would be even greater, and could conceivably do some damage to the ship's skin. The *Enterprise* did have force screens, however, capable of deflecting phaser beams or even photon torpedoes that did not make a direct hit. By turning on the screens, it could deflect enough of the collisions to preserve the outer hull without damage to the ship's occupants.

"What's the maximum speed the *Enterprise* could safely make through that nebula with shields up?" Kirk asked his science officer.

"Considering the ship's coefficient of drag and the skin surface temperature tolerances, I would estimate we could travel at Warp 5.8."

Kirk frowned. They were going at Warp 7 now. The question was whether the shorter distance to travel would more than compensate for their loss in speed. "And the time it would take along a straight-line course from our present position to Epsilon Delta 4 at that speed?"

Spock had it all figured. "Approximately 4.087 days, Captain."

That was a savings of almost an entire day from the current estimate. Kirk felt a warm glow spread through his chest with the knowledge that once again he had tackled a difficult problem and made the answer come out the way he wanted it.

There would be other dangers inside the nebula,

of course. There were no stars apparent within the cloud, but other dangers could be concealed within it. Nebulae like this were the breeding grounds of stars, and there was always the chance of running into a little glowing knot of incandescence that was just on its way to starhood. Asteroids and other debris were sometimes known to occupy the space within a gaseous nebula, although the ship's deflectors could handle anything up to the size of a small moon.

It should be all right if we keep a careful watch to make sure we don't run into anything, Kirk thought, quite pleased with himself. Aloud, he said, "Mr. Sulu, override the computer avoidance program and lay in a straight-line course for Epsilon Delta 4. Proceed at Warp 5.8, shields up. And I want our forward sensors on maximum range for a full scan of 180 degrees; if there's anything out there larger than a pea, I want to know about it instantly."

5

Captain's Log, Stardate 6191.7:

(First Officer Spock reporting)

It has now been two days since Captain Kirk ordered the ship through the region of nebulosity
rather than detouring around the navigational hazard
as is standard procedure. Though he and I have been
standing alternating six-hour watches, the interval
has been refreshingly free of troublesome incidents.
Barring unforseen circumstances, the *Enterprise*
will reach Epsilon Delta 4 in two more days. Chief
Engineer Scott informs me that all systems will be
properly functioning for the emergency evacuation
by that time. In all, I can report that conditions
aboard ship are exactly what they should be under
the given circumstances.

The Bridge was quiet as Spock sat calmly in the
command chair. Though most of the people on duty
at the moment were from the second or third shift,
they were all more than capable at their jobs and they
knew Spock's preference for quiet efficiency. There
was little joking or personal byplay as there sometimes
was when the captain was in this chair; although there

was no concrete evidence that such behavior detract-
ed from efficiency, Spock disapproved of anything
that took the crew's attention away from the performance of their duties.

Spock liked a quiet Bridge—it gave him that much
more time to think. Unfortunately, the Bridge of the
Enterprise was seldom as quiet as he would have
preferred; the very nature of the ship's mission was
to seek out the unique and the unusual, which frequently led to trouble and disquieting activities.
Spock would not avoid trouble if it confronted him,
but neither did he seek it out. That was not always
the case, he felt, with his captain; at times it seemed
as though James Kirk actually went to great lengths
to ensure that the *Enterprise* would see more than
the optimum share of excitement.

The current situation was a case in point. To Spock,
there was no logical reason why the *Enterprise* had
to be placed in a position of danger by traveling
through this nebula. The saving of one day from the
total duration of their trip would make little if any
difference to the success of their mission; the argon
poisoning was such a slow-acting phenomenon that
none of the colonists was likely to die of an extra
day's exposure. If Spock had been commanding the
vessel, he would have weighed the time gained by
the shortcut against the possible harm to the ship by
traveling through uncharted territory and decided
against taking the extra risk.

But that was where he and his captain differed.
Kirk was a man with a strong flair for the dramatic,
and even Spock had to admit that Kirk was at his
absolute best when the element of danger was present
in whatever he was doing. This shortcut, while pointless in its overall effect, would be symbolic to Kirk
of a triumph against nature; and Terrans, Spock had
noticed, were particularly influenced by such petty
symbolism.

When they had first entered the nebula the temperature of the hull had increased dramatically, even with the shields up. Spock had kept a very close eye on the increasing heat, ready to inform the captain the instant critical tolerances were reached. Fortunately, the temperature climb had evened out shortly before the critical level, just as Spock had calculated it would, so there was no actual reason to cease the traveling through the nebula and return to normal space.

Since then, there had been little trouble. The *Enterprise* had encountered small pieces of cosmic debris along its route, the largest being a meteoroid nearly a kilometer in diameter. They could avoid the larger objects with ease, while the smaller ones grazed effortlessly off the shields almost as though they didn't exist at all. It was beginning to look as though the captain's gamble had paid off once more, and Mr. Spock was currently speculating about the nature of luck and why James Kirk seemed to have more of it than most other people he'd met.

The helmsman's sharp cry broke his mild reverie. "Mr. Spock, sensor readings show something dead ahead!"

Spock was instantly alert as his computerlike mind raced through the priorities of action. His first move was to press the intercom button that would connect him with the captain's quarters, where Kirk was sleeping during the off-shift. "Captain Kirk, to the Bridge," he said tersely. "Helmsman reports sighting of a potential obstacle." Kirk had left standing orders that he was to be notified the instant anything was detected.

That act accomplished, Spock turned back to the helmsman. "Lieutenant Rodrigues, what is the nature of the obstacle?"

"Sensors show an incredible outpouring of energy."

"A star?"

"No, sir, not quite like anything I've ever seen before. It's coming up awfully fast, though; the instruments show it's approaching us at several times our own speed."

"Alter course fifteen degrees to starboard, Lieutenant."

"Aye aye, sir." Rodrigues expertly punched the instructions into his navigational computer, and the ship responded instantly. There was the gentle push of a sideways acceleration as the ship veered slightly from its original path.

Without turning in his seat, Spock aimed a remark over his shoulder at Ensign Chekov, who was currently manning the science console where Spock himself would normally be stationed. "Mr. Chekov, I want detailed readings on this energy source, including distribution curve and . . ."

"Sir!" Rodrigues interrupted. His voice was sharp and slightly edged with panic. "The obstacle has shifted course along with us, and is still coming straight at the ship. It . . . it seems to be getting faster all the time."

Spock recognized the incipient hysteria in Rodrigues's voice, and was determined to quash any such outbreak of emotion before it could do any damage. Panic on the Bridge must be avoided at all costs; even Captain Kirk, for all his blatant emotionalism, recognized that fact. "Indeed, Lieutenant?" he said in a voice as dry as he could manage. For emphasis, he lifted an eyebrow as he gazed calmly at the helmsman. "That could very well indicate some artificial nature to this phenomenon. Put a view up on the forward screen so we may all examine it."

The coolness of Spock's voice had its desired effect; Rodrigues was once again all business as he worked his controls. Within seconds, the forward screen image shifted to reveal the obstacle that was rapidly closing with the *Enterprise*.

"Most peculiar," Spock muttered half under his breath—and, as usual, it was an understatement.

Everyone on the Bridge stared at the sight before them. Against the dark background of interstellar space—almost barren of stars because of the obscuring nebular material through which they were passing—was a shining filament that grew noticeably larger with each passing second. It appeared to be nothing less than an enormous rift, a tear in the very fabric of space. Through the opening, the crew could see tantalizing glimpses of *something* that seemed to be of another universe altogether. This hole in reality was speeding toward them at a rate totally uncharacteristic of natural objects.

To test the rift still further, Mr. Spock said calmly, "Return to original course, Mr. Rodrigues."

As the lieutenant worked his controls, the *Enterprise* shifted its course back fifteen degrees to port. The rift disappeared from the forward screen momentarily, then suddenly reappeared even closer than before. "The thing has shifted back, too, Mr. Spock!"

"So I see." Again, Spock refused to be perturbed. "Cut power, Mr. Rodrigues. Let's see what it does when we stop."

A ship the size of the *Enterprise,* massing 190,000 metric tons and traveling at Warp 5.8, could not come to a dead stop instantaneously. Nevertheless, it had been designed for intricate battlefield maneuvering, where almost any command might be necessary. In a short time, the *Enterprise* was almost literally stopped in its tracks, and hung suspended in space before the onrushing hyperspacial rift.

But, as was obvious from the forward screens, that did not deter the forward motion of the strange obstacle before them. If anything, the rift only seemed encouraged by the ship's maneuver, and accelerated still further.

Whatever it was, it was behaving exactly like a predator chasing its prey. It wanted the *Enterprise*—and just as surely, Spock wanted to avoid that. "Full speed astern," he ordered.

Lieutenant Rodrigues remained frozen at his spot, mesmerized by the approaching image of the rift. Spock was tempted to leap out of his seat and work the controls himself, but he decided to let his voice do the work for him. "*Now*, Mr. Rodrigues."

Though his tone was no louder than he had used before, there was such an air of authority behind it that Rodrigues jumped as though stung by the crack of a whip. He worked the appropriate controls to put the massive battle cruiser into reverse at once. The entire ship underwent a massive jolt, and those crew members not on the Bridge, unaware of precisely what was happening, were startled and badly shaken by the experience.

Unfortunately, Spock could not allow them the time to speculate on what was occuring. Even as the ship jumped backward, his long, slender forefinger had depressed the Red Alert button that started the warning horns blaring throughout the ship. The crew, many of whom had been preparing the *Enterprise* for upcoming evacuation, now had to drop whatever they were doing and run to their battle stations at top paring to fight.

Spock watched the viewscreens impassively. The rift had continued to accelerate, and even the reverse motion would be far short of what was needed to escape it. Still, there was no sign of the slightest emotion on his Vulcan countenance.

He had been loathe to use offensive weapons. The *Enterprise*'s mission was to make peaceful contacts with other life forms, and the rift's motions had shown indication of intelligence behind it. But escape was impossible, and there was no time to open channels of communications. The rift would be upon them in a matter of seconds unless something was done. "Phaser banks ready," he said evenly. "Lock onto target and fire at will, immediately."

The phaser banks of the *U.S.S. Enterprise*, the most lethal firepower the Federation could build into a mobile structure, fired their deadly energies into the gaping hole that was bearing down upon them with such fantastic speed. But those weapons, capable of leveling whole cities in a single sweep, had no effect on the oncoming phenomenon. The energy beams just vanished into the nothingness beyond the rift.

"I should have known," Spock muttered, so low that only he could hear it. "You can't *shoot* a hole."

The rift was almost upon them now, with no hope of escaping it. With one smooth gesture of his finger, Mr. Spock turned on the general intercom so that his voice would reach every member of the crew. "Collision with unknown phenomenon is imminent. Prepare for—"

And without further warning, blackness overtook the *Enterprise*.

Captain Kirk had been sleeping when Spock's call came in. Since diverting the ship's course through the nebula, he had been grabbing every hour of sleep he could. The watch duty which he alternated with his first officer was quiet, but a strain nonetheless; passing through a hazardous region left little margin for error, and every sense had to be alert for the slightest sign of trouble. Under normal circumstances a junior watch officer could take command of the Bridge during noncritical times, leaving the captain and the first officer a little more spare time for relaxation; but now every moment was critical, and Kirk could not trust anyone other than Spock and himself to be in command.

He came instantly awake as Spock's voice called into his room, summoning him to the Bridge to investigate a possible obstacle; the ability to pass from sleep to full wakefulness was one that most great military men learned at some point during their early careers, and it was an ability that Kirk valued highly.

He rolled out of bed and quickly dressed in the fresh uniform he had laid out beside the bed before going to sleep. His stomach was rumbling, but he would not take time now to grab even a quick snack; he could always have something brought to the Bridge if his presence was needed there for more than just a few moments. *It's my own fault for leaving orders to notify me if anything happens,* he thought cynically. *It's probably just another little chunk of rock. But better safe than sorry.*

He had just started out of his cabin when he was jolted twice—first by the ship's coming to a stop, and then by the change into reverse. *What in hell's going on up there?* he wondered. Moments later, horns started blaring and lights began flashing throughout the ship's corridors. Red alert! So much for his supposition that the obstacle was merely a small chunk of rock. If a Vulcan thought the situation called for a red alert, things must be critical indeed.

Kirk broke into a run toward the turbolift. He was needed on the Bridge *now;* there was no time to lose. Even as he raced down the hallway he could hear the high-pitched whine of the phaser banks firing at some unknown target. His mind conjured up a dozen horrifying fantasies as he tried to imagine what situation could cause Mr. Spock, a normally calm officer who preferred peaceful solutions to most problems, to fire the ship's weapons so quickly and so willfully.

He had almost reached the door of the turbolift when Spock's voice came over the loudspeaker: "Collision with unknown phenomenon is imminent. Prepare for—"

Then blackness, and a loss of gravity, and silence as well—a total sensory deprivation that left Kirk feeling as though he had dropped out of existence into some nightmarish limbo. His momentum carried him against the forward wall with a crash, and instinctively he reached out for a handhold to stop his motion.

The silence was not quite total; all the other people aboard the ship were still alive. Kirk could hear scattered sounds down the corridor, and a couple of people calling to one another through the darkness. The reason the silence had seemed so blanketing at first was that all the little shipboard sounds—the blowing of the ventilators, the tiny humming of the machines —all those had vanished along with the lights and the artificial gravity. To Kirk, that signified one thing: loss of power, on this level at least if not aboard the entire ship.

To test his theory, he pushed off gently from his perch and floated toward the turbolift. The doors should have parted for him automatically; instead, he bumped into them. The power was definitely out on Deck Five.

There were backup systems that should have cut in within seconds; the fact that they didn't only indicated that there was something more seriously wrong. Perhaps Scotty's engineers had been working on the emergency backup systems when the crisis hit—the epitome of poor timing. Or perhaps the disaster that had befallen the *Enterprise* was so vast in scope that even the backups were unequal to the task.

If that were the case . . . Kirk hated to think about all the problems a complete lack of power throughout the ship would cause. In total darkness, even Scotty himself would be hard put to repair anything—and within just a couple of hours all the air would start going bad. The crew would die from asphyxiation long before they could die of thirst or starvation.

More than ever, Kirk felt that his presence was needed on the Bridge. Somehow, he had a mystical feeling that no problem was insoluble as long as he was there. It was his own personal place of power, the source of his inspiration. But the Bridge was four decks away, and the turbolifts were not working; he would have to find an alternate route.

So attuned was Kirk with his ship that he knew his way through most of it by feel alone. Keeping his hands along the wall as a guide, he turned back in the direction he'd come and began swimming through the air at a deliberate pace. He forced himself not to rush, not to panic; there would be plenty of time to do whatever needed doing if he didn't lose his head.

He counted off the various doors as he passed them, picturing each in his mind's eye and comparing them to his memory of where each should be in relation to his destination. At last he came to the door he wanted, the exit to the emergency stairwell. During normal conditions, this door was sealed tight with a magnetic lock run by the same circuits that ran the turbolift; if those circuits ever failed, the magnetic lock would also fail, allowing the stairs to be used. It was an ingenious failsafe mechanism, and it served its purpose well; the emergency door opened easily at Kirk's touch.

Despite the fact that air normally circulated here as well as anywhere else aboard the ship, the stairway still had a musty smell of disuse about it. Kirk moved carefully, trying to avoid collisions, as he groped blindly for the handrail. He finally found it and, gripping it tightly, he swam slowly into the darkness. As long as the railing on his right was spiralling clockwise he knew he was going in the right direction; there was no other way to tell that he was going "up" instead of "down."

He counted the levels by the number of landings he passed as he ascended. He needn't have bothered; it was obvious when he reached the Bridge. Mr. Spock's calm voice could be heard even through the closed door, fully in charge of the situation. Kirk, for perhaps the millionth time, thanked God and Star Fleet for giving him such a competent first officer; few other people could have staved off panic half as well as that tall, emotionless Vulcan.

Spock was in the process of re-establishing communications despite the loss of power as Kirk quietly opened the door to the Bridge. "People communicated with one another all the time before the advent of electricity, Lieutenant Leaming," the Vulcan was explaining dryly. "If necessary, we can find a pipe that leads down to Engineering and beat on it in code until they reply."

"Or we can set up a system of tom-toms," Kirk said.

The effect of his voice on the people within the chamber was electric. There were a few intakes of breath as the Bridge crew realized that their captain was somehow miraculously among them once more. Even Spock sounded relieved as he said, "It's good to hear that you've made it back to us, Captain. I presume you took the emergency stairway."

"Yes, the power's out on Deck Five. Is it out all over the ship?"

"It appears to be—although without the power to check, it's impossible to determine from here. And, of course, it is difficult to reach Engineering for a fuller report."

"What happened? One moment we were sailing along smoothly, the next we'd gone to red alert."

Spock filled his superior in on the events that had taken place since the initial discovery of the spacial rift. He delivered the story in his usual flat tones, but Kirk could imagine the desperation his people on the Bridge faced as that hole in space bore down relentlessly upon them.

When the first officer had finished, Kirk paused to consider the situation. "The logical assumption, then," he said at last, "is that we have traveled through that rift, and are now in some totally different universe—perhaps even one in which physical laws as we know them don't apply. That would explain why the power went out suddenly."

"A little too general an assumption, Captain. Some physical laws work, or our bodies themselves would cease to function. We continue to breathe, indicating that the chemical processes of respiration are operating normally. The electrical synapses in our brains have not been noticeably affected. Sound waves travel through the air in the standard manner. The cohesion between the cells continues to hold our bodies together. All these things and more prove that physical laws do indeed apply as they used to; it is only our power systems that have been affected."

"There's certainly nothing wrong with the way your logic is working," Kirk grinned, even though no one could see the expression. "All right, then as far as we know only our power systems are out. That's enough of an emergency for me, anyway.

"Our first priority, as you were discussing when I entered, is to regain communication with Engineering so we can find out what's wrong. After that, the most important thing is to get the air circulating again through the ship—maybe Scotty can rig up some manual pumps. Once the air's moving, we'll have to find some way to work the filters and recyclers manually so we'll have oxygen to breathe instead of carbon dioxide. Then we . . ."

Kirk got no further in his listing of priorities as the lights and the gravity came on abruptly once more. The men and women of the crew, who had been floating at their stations, fell to the floor in a series of bumps. No one seemed seriously hurt, but all were startled. The sudden brightness hurt their eyes and they blinked back tears as they tried to become accustomed to the lights again. After a moment of silence, there was a loud spontaneous cheer that echoed through the Bridge—and, Kirk was willing to bet, throughout the rest of the ship as well.

Taking long strides, he moved to the communications console and punched the intercom for Engineering. "Scotty, I don't know what you did, but it worked."

The chief engineer's voice drifted up to them. "I canna take the credit, Captain; I dinna know what I did, either. We were workin' in the dark, literally, not quite knowin' what was wrong in the first place when all of a sudden the power came on by itself."

"Perhaps we passed through an area of magnetic anomaly," Spock suggested. "We should take our bearings and find out exactly where we are."

Kirk turned back to the forward screen, hoping to make some sense of the starfield that should have been there—but as he saw what the screen showed, he froze in amazement. Others among the crew, seeing the captain's reaction, also turned toward the screen—and they, too were startled by what they saw.

"A very good point, Mr. Spock," Kirk said when he regained his voice. "We obviously went through that rift and came out here. But where, exactly, is *here?*

6

What the crew of the *Enterprise* expected to see on the screen was the blackness of interstellar space —a blackness penetrated only by the handful of stars bright enough to shine through the obscuring nebula through which the ship had been traveling. Instead, they saw ahead of them a milky glow of rainbow luminescence, dazzling to the eyes, changing colors in a continuous, kaleidoscopic display. It was as though someone had crushed a billion pearls and painted them on the screen with a bright spotlight behind them shifting angles every few seconds.

"Mr. Spock," Kirk said quietly, "I want some readings. Find out where we are and what that . . . *stuff* is out there." The only thing similar that Kirk had ever experienced was the energy barrier that surrounded the Galaxy, through which the *Enterprise* had passed on a couple of occasions. That barrier had caused problems to the ship before; if this was anything remotely related to it, he wanted to know about it quickly.

While Spock was at work bending over his instruments, Kirk called for a systems check all over the ship. Each department in turn gave him a status report, and each was almost identical with the one that preceded it: the only problem had been the disruption of power and now, with that condition alleviated, everything was working perfectly. The *Enterprise* had never been in better shape.

Kirk, who tended to be suspicious of news that was *too* good, scowled. It didn't make sense. He was about to find, though, that many things in this locale did not make much sense.

Spock had finished his preliminary investigation by the time the status reports were completed. "It seems, Captain, that in passing through that rift we did indeed pass through a hole in space. We are now in a place *beyond* space, for lack of a better word. It is like a bubble suspended in a fluid of greater density. The bubble is approximately spherical, with a mean diameter of 3.7 light years. It is filled, not with the vacuum we normally associate with our own interplanetary void, but with a unique form of energy —again, words fail. I would describe it as liquid energy, energy that is drifting free all around us in a potential form, ready to be utilized by anyone or anything that knows how."

"Is it anything like the force barrier around our galaxy?" Kirk asked.

"It does bear a superficial resemblance; I would hazard that the two types of force are related in some way, but this one is not nearly so menacing in its application."

"Still, it has a potential we must keep in mind," Kirk mused. Turning to the communications console, he faced Lieutenant Leaming who was handling that aspect of ship function while Lieutenant Uhura was off duty. "Lieutenant, see if we can get a message out through the rift we entered—"

"Don't bother, Captain," Spock said. "The rift has apparently sealed up again now that we are inside this bubble. I could find no trace of an opening during my examination."

"Then try other subspace channels," Kirk continued to the communications officer. "We must attempt to let Star Fleet know what's happened to us. If we can't find our way out of this soon, they'll have to dispatch another ship to evacuate Epsilon Delta 4."

He turned back to Spock. "You said this area had a definite size. That implies walls, a boundary of some sort to hold it in. We came through it once, perhaps we can get out the same way."

"I do not know, Captain," Spock said with a shrug. "There are still so many unknown factors. In theory there must be a way out if there's a way in, but in practice..."

"It's worth a try at least. Even if we end up disabled once more, at least we'll be back in normal space where we know what to expect. Ahead Warp Factor 1, Mr. Rodrigues."

"Aye aye, sir." The helmsman set the appropriate instructions into his computer and waited to confirm the readouts. After studying his screen for several seconds, he tried the controls once more. "Sir, something peculiar is happening. Computer acknowledges instructions, but the sensors give no speed reading."

Kirk frowned and pressed the intercom button. "Engineering. Scotty, is something wrong with the engines?"

The engineer's voice sounded bemused. "The engines are all workin' perfectly, Captain. It's just that we're not movin'."

"A contradiction in terms," Spock muttered under his breath.

"Try impulse power, Mr. Rodrigues," Kirk said.

This time the maneuver met with more success. "Impulse power works, Captain," the helmsman reported, "but much slower than normal."

"If this is the fastest we can go," Spock commented from his position, "it will take us almost a week to reach the nearest wall of our bubble. And, at this speed, it is most doubtful that we would have enough momentum to burst through."

Kirk cursed under his breath and had the helmsman try again at various combinations of warp speed. It was all to no avail. The fastest the *Enterprise* could manage to travel within this strange environment was a slow crawl.

"Sir!" It was Chekov, now, reporting from the navigator's chair where he'd gone after Spock relieved him at the science console. "Sensors indicate another vessel in the immediate area."

Kirk peered at the forward screen, but it was almost impossible to see anything through the strange pearlescent fog. "Location, Mr. Chekov?"

"Bearing 208.34, range 148,000 kilometers."

"Relative velocity?"

"Not appreciable, sir."

Kirk mulled on that for a moment. Whatever this other ship was, it was very far away and apparently as motionless as the *Enterprise*. But was it friend or foe? Had it, like the *Enterprise*, found itself trapped here—or was it the cause of the *Enterprise's* current predicament? "Analysis, Mr. Spock?"

The science officer consulted his instruments. "Some large form of star cruiser, similar to ours. Its mass is equivalent, and I can detect radiation similar to what we would expect from a ship that operates on the matter-antimatter principle. More detailed analysis is not possible at this time because of the object's extreme range and the obstructive effects of the local environment."

"Thank you." Kirk turned to the communications officer. "Any luck contacting Star Fleet yet?"

"Negative, sir," the lieutenant replied. "All I get is echoes of our own message, as though the walls of this place are bouncing it back at us."

"Switch to hailing frequencies, then, and see if we can contact this other ship."

After a moment, Lieutenant Leaming replied, "They acknowledge our signal, Captain."

"Good. Send this message: 'This is the *U.S.S. Enterprise*, Captain James Kirk commanding. Please identify yourself.'"

The response that came back a few moments later, though, was neither expected nor particularly welcome. The view of pearly nothingness on the forward screen faded out, to be replaced by a harsh, swarthy face with thick, bifurcated eyebrows and short-cut black hair. "This is the Klingon Star Cruiser *Destructor,* commanded by Captain Kolvor. I demand an immediate explanation for this outrage."

It's not bad enough having to be stuck in a place like this, Kirk thought with dismay. *But having to be stuck in here with a Klingon . . . and a belligerent one, at that.*

Although, he was quick to add, *there aren't any other kinds.*

"Outrage?" he asked aloud.

"Yes. My ship was peacefully pursuing its business —well within the confines of our borders, I might add —when we were swooped down upon by this diabolical new weapon of the Federation's and imprisoned here against our will. This is a clear violation of the Organian Peace Treaty, and you can believe that full mention of it will be made upon our return to base."

"I assure you, Captain, that we are in the same predicament. Whatever this phenomenon is, it is none of our doing. We're trapped here, the same as you. Perhaps if we were to pool our data and our resources, we might come up with an explanation or solution. Please state your current situation."

The Klingon's eyes narrowed suspiciously. The thought of working with a member of the hated Federation did not sit well with him. "All ship's functions are performing normally."

"The odds are he's lying, Captain," Spock advised quietly so that his voice would not be picked up and broadcast to the enemy ship. "Klingons are much more prone to actions than words. If his ship were capable of moving, I assume it would be doing so by now. He is probably frozen the same as we are."

Kirk nodded in agreement. The Klingon was reluctant to admit his ship's disability to the Terran—and Kirk himself had to admit he was less than enthusiastic about telling the other that he was stuck, too. In the confrontations that often evolved between Federation and Klingon forces, it was not the best policy to expose your weaknesses to the other side.

He was about to try framing a diplomatic reply when another exclamation from Ensign Chekov cut him off. "Sensors now show another ship in the area, Captain. Bearing 143.17, range 113,000 kilometers."

"Excuse me for a moment, Captain Kolvor," Kirk said. "Someone else seems to have joined our party."

"So I have been informed." Kolvor's smile held little mirth and less warmth. Kirk gave a nod to Lieutenant Leaming, and the Klingon's image faded from the screen, to be replaced once again by the strange glow of their environment.

"Can you give me any information about this new ship, Spock?" Kirk asked.

"No more than I could concerning the Klingon vessel. Smaller mass, similar radiation pattern. Whatever this bubble is that we are in, it seems to be gobbling up star cruisers."

An idea flashed through Kirk's mind. "Would you care to bet that this newcomer is a Romulan, Mr. Spock?"

"I prefer not to gamble, Captain, particularly when the odds are so high against being correct. Of all the possible ships in the Galaxy, the chances are against its being any one particular nationality. Why do you suppose otherwise?"

"Just a hunch. Whoever or whatever is behind this has gathered in one Federation vessel and one Klingon vessel. Why not get a Romulan vessel as well and then have a delegation from each of the three major powers in the Galaxy?"

"You are assuming an intelligent force acting behind these events. That has yet to be conclusively determined."

"Nevertheless, I put my money on a Romulan. Lieutenant Leaming, open a channel and see what happens."

Lieutenant Leaming turned back to the communications panel and did as instructed. Within a few moments, another face appeared on the forward screen: a face with the cold eyes and Vulcanoid ears of a Romulan. Kirk turned to give Spock an I-told-you-so glance, but the first officer's only reaction was to blink calmly and keep his gaze focused on the screen. Cheated of his triumph, Kirk turned back to business.

Again, formal introductions were exchanged. The Romulan leader was Commander Actius Probicol, and his ship was the *Talon*. Like the other two ships, his had been about its own business when it was suddenly swooped down upon by the transspacial rift and found itself within this bubble of unreality. He refused to give any more information than that, however, and when Kirk pressed, the Romulan broke off communications.

"Three ships in a small volume of space," Kirk mused aloud. "All intact and unable to move." A sudden thought occurred to him, and he jabbed the intercom button. "Scotty, can you test our weapons without firing them?"

"Aye, Captain."

"Then please do it now. We may be in for a fight, but if we start firing first the other two will certainly take it as a belligerent move and combine against us." He turned back to Spock. "The problem is that both of them are our enemies, but we don't know exactly how they feel about each other. We know there's some sort of trade agreement so that the Klingons supply the Romulans with ships, but whether that agreement is also a mutual defense pact remains to be seen."

"There is no record," said Spock, "of any Klingon fighting on behalf of the Romulans, or vice versa."

"I'd hate to set a precedent," Kirk said glumly.

At that moment, Scotty reported back. "All our tests show that the weapons *should* work—but until we fire 'em, we canna be sure. They may be like the engines, that work perfectly but dinna do anything."

"Thanks, Scotty."

"I submit, Captain," said Spock, "that if our weapons don't work, then the Klingon and Romulan weapons probably won't either. What is true for one in this bubble seems to be true for all."

"Still, they do outnumber us two to one, and I don't like those odds. I wonder if that's the idea. Whoever is behind this bizarre little game may have brought us all here to see what we'd do—whether we'd cooperate with one another or fight among ourselves until only one side was left."

"Really, Captain, you slander me," came a strange voice from the front of the chamber. "I had no such bloodthirsty motivations at all."

7

There was a gnome standing on the Bridge of the *Enterprise* just in front of the forward screen. He could not have been more than a meter tall, with curly brown hair and a trim black goatee and mustache. To judge by his apparel, he had dressed in the dark: a bright red satin shirt with silver embroidered designs; deep purple velvet knee britches with a pink kidskin belt; orange socks; gold slippers whose toes curved upward in outrageous curlicues; and, topping the ensemble, a pointed chartreuse cap with a little bell on the top. The weight of the bell made the point of the cap tilt over to one side at a cockeyed angle.

The crew on the Bridge could only stare at this apparition in silence for several stunned seconds. The gnome, in turn, stared back at them with an equal amount of curiosity, if less surprise. Finally Captain Kirk found his tongue. "Who are you?" he asked.

"My name is Enowil," said the gnome, as though that explained everything.

"And you claim to be responsible for bringing us here?" Mr. Spock asked.

Enowil smiled. "Any sensible man would avoid claims during months that have an 'R' in them."

Spock merely looked perplexed at this reply, so

Kirk interpreted. "It's a pun, Mr. Spock, and not a terribly good one. Besides, it really should be oysters."

"Apparently our tastes in seafood differ, Captain," the gnome responded. "But I will admit that so far, our conversation has been fruitless; perhaps we should continue it at a later date."

At least three separate pun-oriented rejoinders leaped into Kirk's mind, but he quashed them mercilessly. This was no time to play word games. "Enowil," he said, speaking calmly and distinctly, "we have been transported to this . . . place against our will. We do not know why or how, or what will become of us. If you have any knowledge of these events, we would be most grateful if you'd enlighten us."

"I am hurt, though, by your supposition that I brought you and the others here to fight. In all my many millennia of existence, I have never intentionally been the cause of harm to even the tiniest of living creatures." The gnome pouted childishly.

Kirk took a deep breath. He could see that this situation would require his utmost patience and diplomatic skill. "I am very sorry I cast aspersions upon your character. You must realize that I was facing a strange situation, and I am responsible for the welfare of the hundreds of people aboard my ship. I had to fear the worst. Now that I've met you, I can see that you obviously mean us no harm."

"No one can harm the man who himself does no wrong."

"Uh, yes. Nevertheless, we find ourselves in an unusual position and we were wondering what you could do to help us understand what is happening. For instance," Kirk said, picking a minor example to start with, "how did you get here?"

"Ah yes, how does any of us get here?" Enowil said, his eyes lighting up. "I had no idea you were a metaphysician, Captain."

"I meant here on the Bridge, specifically."

"Oh, that." His face fell again. "It's simple enough, really. I can do anything, you see. At least, here within this bubble. I can do quite a lot outside it, too, but why bother? This is enough of a world for me."

Although Kirk tended to doubt the extravagance of the claim, he was careful not to show any reaction. Instead he continued calmly, "Why were we brought here?"

"Because I need your help."

"I thought you said you could do anything," Mr. Spock interrupted. "If that is the case, what could we possibly do for you that you cannot do for yourself?"

Enowil turned to look at him. "Oh good, you were paying attention. I dislike having to repeat myself; it becomes so *iterative*, if you know what I mean. Just keep everything in mind and I'm sure you'll do well on the test afterward. Yes, of course I said I can *do* anything; the problem is that I don't *know* everything. You see, to do is not to know and, conversely, to know is not to do. The difference between action and knowledge is like the difference between . . . well, between having a person *at* your side and *on* your side, don't you see?"

Kirk was trying to cut through the foliage of that last speech to find the meaning hidden in its center. "You mean you need us to supply you with some information," he hazarded.

Enowil clapped his hands with delight. "Oh, you Terrans are so clever. I'm sure you'll have no trouble at all solving my problem."

Lieutenant Rodrigues, who had been watching Enowil more than his console, suddenly looked down at the glowing red lights. "Sir!" he exclaimed. "The Klingons have fired on our ship with photon torpedoes. Impact in fifteen seconds."

"Shields up, quickly," was Kirk's instinctive reaction.

"Oh, those naughty Klingons," Enowil said with a sigh. "What are we to do with them? Excuse me, Captain, I must straighten them out." And with that, the gnome vanished from the Bridge as abruptly as he'd appeared.

"Wait a minute," Kirk said, entirely too late. If Enowil was really as powerful as he claimed to be, he might have been able to prevent damage to the *Enterprise;* but now the Federation crew would have to stand up against the Klingon onslaught on their own devices. The ship was unable to move fast enough to evade the oncoming torpedoes; Kirk would have to rely on the strength of the shields—if they worked at all in this peculiar bubble.

"All hands," Kirk announced over the intercom, "Prepare for torpedo impact."

Kirk braced himself in his chair as the sensors indicated the photon torpedoes were coming nearer the ship. There was a dazzling flash of lights on the forward screen and the crew cringed, prepared for the shaking the ship was certain to take. But nothing further happened. When several seconds had gone by without further incident, the crewmembers opened their eyes again and looked to the screen for explanation.

There, in a blaze of fireworks against the pearlescent background, was a rectangular design of green, red and white sparks—which Kirk recognized belatedly as being a reasonable likeness of the Imperial Klingonese Flag.

Somebody around here, Kirk thought, *has a sense of humor. Since Klingons are notably lacking in that department, I suspect it's our new friend Enowil. But what's his game?*

"Mr. Spock," he said aloud, "how would you describe Enowil's behavior so far?"

"Bizarre, unpredictable, perhaps whimsical, certainly running heavily on emotions. Harmless and friendly so far. But if what he says is true, he has the potential to do great damage to the *Enterprise.*"

"Would you include 'childish' among your list of adjectives?"

"If you mean like a Terran child, yes. The adjective did not come directly to mind because Vulcan children do not behave in quite that manner."

Kirk smiled in spite of himself. He remembered a conversation he'd had with Amanda, Spock's mother —and no matter what Spock said, Kirk doubted that Vulcan children were all that different from their Terran counterparts. But he let the remark pass without comment; there were more important matters to consider.

"Does he remind you of any other 'child' we've run across?" Kirk asked instead.

"You are thinking of Trelane?" Spock raised an eyebrow inquisitively. "An interesting speculation. But Trelane's powers, while enormous, were never quite on the scale that Enowil has demonstrated today."

The "child" to whom he referred was a being called Trelane, the self-styled "Squire of Gothos," who had created on an otherwise uninhabitable world a recreation of an early nineteenth century British nobleman's estate. Because Trelane had appeared to the crew as a fully adult man, they had not realized the psychology behind his wanting them to join in his games; he used them as personal toys, to be shifted around at his discretion. Only when he was on the verge of killing Kirk did his parents intervene, and the crew of the *Enterprise* then learned that Trelane was actually a child by the standards of his ancient and powerful race. It had left the crew far less willing to accept anything just on the basis of its appearance after that.

"It's something we have to keep in mind, though," Kirk said. "He obviously behaves in what we would consider an eccentric manner. We'll have to humor him until we find out exactly what he's after."

He did not have long to wait. Within a few minutes, Enowil reappeared on the Bridge, looking as garish as ever. "I have just spoken with the captains of the other two ships," he said, "and I explained to them that this sort of behavior simply will not be tolerated. Whatever your petty squabbles may be outside, this is my bubble and you're all my guests. I expect you all to maintain at least a basic civility toward one another while you're here."

"You bring up an interesting point," Kirk said. "Exactly how long *will* we be here?"

Enowil cocked his head at a curious angle, and the little bell on top of his cap tinkled slightly as it moved. "That depends," he said. "Hopefully you'll solve my problem very quickly and you'll be off on your business again before you know it."

"What if we are unable to solve your problem?" Spock asked coldly.

"I hadn't really considered that. You're very clever, and I was hoping that you—or the Klingons or the Romulans—would think of something. Still, I would hate the thought of keeping anyone against his will; you could go, I guess. But you wouldn't get the reward."

"Reward?" Kirk asked suspiciously. "What reward?"

"*My* reward, of course; I couldn't very well offer you someone else's, could I? And before you ask, Captain—no, I am not Trelane."

Kirk's mouth fell open. "How—are you a telepath?"

"Not at the moment, though I suppose I could be if I wanted to. But you do have to be careful what you say, Captain. The walls, after all, have ears."

And so they did. Somehow, the walls of the *Enterprise*'s Bridge had sprouted dozens of ears, all sizes and shapes; from tiny baby ears to adult male ears to Vulcan ears to donkey ears—all intently listening to the conversations on the Bridge around them.

"Actually I met Trelane's parents once several centuries ago, but Trelane was only an infant then. Hardly worth knowing," Enowil said, totally ignoring the gasps from the crew.

"An . . . *interesting* child, wouldn't you say?" Kirk asked.

The gnome made a face. "A spoiled brat, if you ask me. Spoil the rod and spare the child, that's what I always say. By the way, Captain, you really should do something about all those ears on the wall—they're disgusting."

"My thoughts exactly," Kirk said. "Could you ... ?"

"My pleasure." The ears were gone and the walls were just walls once more. Enowil had not done so much as wave his hand. "There, that's better. They were much too distracting. I was just about to tell you about my problem, if you're interested."

Kirk was about to say "I'm all ears," but abruptly changed his mind. Instead, he merely replied, "Yes, I'm sure we all are."

"I am—or I was, at least—an Organian. Ah, I see by your face, Captain, that you've heard of us."

Kirk had done more than that; he and the *Enterprise* had actually been to that mysterious planet at one time, when a war between the Federation and the Klingon Empire was imminent. Since Organia occupied a strategic location between the two powers, each side naturally wanted to use it as a base for operations against the other. To all appearances, the Organians were a simple, primitive and pacifistic race, unwilling to offer any resistance when both sides started fighting over them; but again, as was the case with Trelane, appearances were deceiving. In reality, the Organians were a race so far advanced beyond either the Federation or the Klingons that the mortal forms they presented were merely a convenience for the lesser beings they dealt with. Growing at last annoyed by what seemed to them the petty bickering of children, they intervened and stopped the Federation-Klingon war dead in its tracks. Using their superior abilities, they enforced a treaty upon the two sides wherein armed conflict would be replaced by peaceful competition. And, while the Klingons had violated the spirit, if not the actual letter, of the treaty more times than Kirk would care to count, it had at least brought a semblance of peace and order to the Galaxy.

If Enowil was indeed an Organian, Kirk realized he would have to tread much more carefully in this matter. The Organians, while very tolerant of others (up to a point), had their own strict code of behavior to which they rigorously adhered. They were indeed quite powerful and, while Enowil's claim to not harming anyone would be fully justified in that case, the mere presence of so much power could not help but cause complications for all the lesser beings involved.

"Yes," Kirk said simply. "I have been to Organia."

"You mentioned," Spock added, "that you *were* an Organian, past tense. What happened to change that status?"

"My, you are perspicacious, aren't you, Mr. Spock? You don't miss a thing. I can tell you should have no difficulty at all in solving my problem. Yes, I was an Organian until the rest of my fellows kicked me out. Oh, not in so crude a way as you're probably picturing. They didn't hand me an ultimatum or anything so melodramatic as that. They would have tolerated me, I suppose—but have you any idea how tedious it can be to be 'tolerated'? It was plain enough they didn't want me there, so I left."

"Why didn't they want you?" Kirk asked, already pretty sure he knew the answer.

Enowil looked both ways as though to make sure no one would overhear. Then he leaned forward and whispered conspiratorially, "They thought I was mad." The whisper carried quite easily to everyone on the Bridge.

"I can't imagine why."

"Ah, sarcasm is the sour cream of wit, Captain. I, of course, in turn thought them stuffy, pedantic and boring. Can you imagine—they could spend decades, literally, pondering the whichness of why, while I, of course, would be far beyond them pondering the whyness of which. Perhaps I was not so careful about dotting every T and crossing every I, but formal imprecision is good for the soul—and gives steady employment to those who come after you. The corollaries I left behind for them could have occupied them for centuries; they should have been delighted. But did they thank me? Not at all. They were quite relieved when I left."

I understand how they felt, Kirk thought, but said nothing aloud.

"Well, to make a brief story short, I struck out on my own. I knew they would be upset with me if I played around with their real universe, so I just formed my own private little bubble of unreality around me. I've been living here ever since. As long as I leave the outside universe alone, the rest of my people are content to let me be—and I'm happy enough here where I can do anything I want."

"Except that you have a problem," Kirk said.

"There's no need to be vulgar. Of course I have a problem. I *told* you I had a problem. That's why I brought you here, to *solve* my problem."

"But won't the other Organians object? You have interfered with the outside universe by bringing us and the Klingons and the Romulans here."

"Pah, Captain—and again I say, pah! I shan't detain you that long. They won't even notice. Even a month is less than the blink of an eye to them—and you entirely overrate your importance in their overall picture of the universe. If I may be permitted a rather bucolic simile, these three ships are like three steers plucked momentarily from an enormous herd. The Organians can't be concerned over so small a number; they only take action when the entire herd begins to stampede."

"I still fail to see your problem," Spock interposed. "You say that within this bubble you are free to do as you wish; that you have the *power* to do as you wish; and that you have no desire to deal with the outside universe. What then is your problem?"

"Ah, what indeed?" Enowil crossed his legs and "sat" suspended in midair, unconcerned by the seeming impossibility of it. The air was suddenly filled with the soft strain of violins as he continued, "Let me tell you. I have been here for three centuries now, give or take a decade or two, and lately I have begun to feel a . . . a lack of something to my existence. That's the best way I can put it—something that should be present to complete my happiness is missing. I've pondered the problem for well over a century, and I can't put my finger on it. Finally, I decided to call in some outside advisors, as it were, and ask their opinions. That's why you're here. You see, while I can do anything, I'm not sure exactly what to do."

"And you expect us to solve a problem that's been puzzling you for over a century?" Kirk asked.

"But you and your people are so clever; Mr. Spock has already demonstrated that. Is not enlightenment often the child (albeit often illegitimate) of wit and courage? Besides, I may be too close to the problem; I may be overlooking something that is completely obvious to an outsider. What have you got to lose except a little time?"

"That's just it—we will lose time. Unfortunately, you picked a less than opportune moment to bring us here. Our ship was on an important mission of mercy, and this delay may well cost hundreds of lives." Kirk went into detail explaining to Enowil about the argon poisoning on Epsilon Delta 4, and how the *Enterprise* was needed to evacuate the planet. Kirk stressed the humanitarian nature of their mission, hoping that Enowil would possess at least the moral sense of the rest of his race.

"Therefore," he concluded, "although we would normally love to help you, we're caught in a bind. I think even you'll admit that your situation is less critical than that of the colonists on Epsilon Delta 4. Won't you please let us return to the mission we'd already begun?"

"You haven't been paying attention, Captain; if you had, you'd know I already answered that question. Sloppy of you. I bet Mr. Spock remembers." Enowil tilted his head in Spock's direction.

"If you remember, Captain, Enowil mentioned earlier that he would not hold anyone here against his will, and that we would be free to go if we chose."

"Excellent!" Enowil clapped his hands, then unfolded his legs so that he was once again standing on solid ground. "You did that very well, Mr. Spock. I'm going to give you a gold star for that. You, Captain, did not learn your lesson nearly as well. You can hardly expect me to give you a gold star for your performance, can you?"

"Then we're free to go? No tricks?"

Enowil looked hurt. "Do I look that cruel? Do you think I would actually stand in the way of your rescuing six hundred and eighty people? I admit to being eccentric, Captain, but I'm no monster." He took off the pointed cap and held it over his heart to emphasize his words. "The fate of those people concerns me deeply. If you'd like, I could even let you out of the bubble right above their planet, to save you further travel time. Why don't you talk it over with the rest of your officers and give me your decision in an hour?"

Kirk had faced too many menaces to view such generosity with anything but suspicion. "And if we decide to go, you'll put us where we want to be, with no catch?"

"No catch." Enowil put his hat back on his head and made a crossing motion over his heart. "The generous man benefits the whole world, while the vindictive man cheats only himself. Do you like that? I spent some time on your home planet once, several centuries ago," he explained. "I was the head writer for a fortune cookie factory.

"Of course," he added offhandedly, "if you leave, you become ineligible for the reward I'd planned to offer the group that solves my problem."

"That's the second time you've mentioned a reward," Kirk said, his eyes narrowing. "What exactly did you plan to give as a prize?"

"Why, anything you want, Captain," Enowil said with a broad smile. "Anything within my power to give, that is. And I must admit, with all undue modesty, that my power is quite considerable indeed."

8

Captain's Log, Stardate 6191.9:

The Organian calling himself Enowil has granted
me an hour to confer with my officers on whether
we should help him solve his problem or whether we
should continue on with our original mission to
evacuate the Epsilon Delta 4 colony. Although he
claimed it hurt his feelings to be suspected, I did
make Enowil promise not to eavesdrop on the meeting—and I believe him to be a being of his word.

I've called together my major officers: Commander
Spock, Lieutenant Commander Scott, and Dr. Mc-
Coy. Also, though she will have no part in the actual
decision, I have allowed Metika Spyroukis to attend
the meeting. The decision made there will, after all,
affect both her and her planet.

With his three most important officers and Metika
Spyroukis present, Kirk called the meeting to order.
Only Spock, of those in the Briefing Room, had any
idea of what was going on, and Kirk did his best to
recount briefly the events that had just transpired on
the ship's Bridge. He was not sure, though, whether
any short description would capture the full "flavor"
of the being they were dealing with.

"Jim," said McCoy when the captain had finished,

"if you want the expert opinion of a physician who has also dabbled in space psychology and mental disorders, I'd have to say that this Enowil is a stark raving looney. I'm surprised the other Organians let him go; if he were any patient of mine I'd have had him carted off to the silly cell a long time ago."

"And yet, Doctor," said Spock, "he is being, in his own eccentric way, quite cooperative. He has neither harmed us nor threatened to; he has said he would let us continue on our previous mission if we desire, and has even offered to help us by taking us to Epsilon Delta 4 immediately."

"You must admit, Bones," Kirk added, "that if we weren't in the middle of an emergency mission, the problem Enowil poses would offer us a fascinating challenge."

"But we *are* on an emergency mission," Metika spoke up. "The Epsilon Delta 4 colony is in trouble. They're my friends down there, close to seven hundred people who may die unless we can evacuate them soon."

"I have to agree with her, Jim," McCoy said. "Each minute we delay, the argon poisoning is reaching higher levels within the bodies of those colonists. They probably haven't reached the danger level yet —but our primary duty is to save their lives, not to play games with some godlike lunatic. I can't even see why you had to call this meeting; the decision is obvious."

"Is it?" Kirk posed the question quietly, but his tone indicated there was something behind it. "Maybe you're forgetting what Enowil said about a reward."

At the end of the table, Metika's mouth dropped open with surprise. She gazed across at the captain for a long moment before speaking. "I can't believe I heard that. My father served in Star Fleet for over half a century, and I was raised to think that Star Fleet people were dedicated to high principles. I thought you lived up to those ideals of service. I never thought I would hear any captain in the Fleet even consider abandoning people in trouble merely for the sake of his own greed."

Kirk looked hurt by her remarks, but it was Spock who answered the charges. "It is not greed, Miss Spyroukis, but practicality."

Metika snorted. "I'd like to hear the rationalization behind that."

Kirk cleared his throat. "Very well. Enowil has offered a reward to whoever can solve his problem—anything that is within his power to give. I've seen evidence of that power, it's incredible. All right, suppose we turn him down, say 'Thank you, but we have other things to do.' What then? The Klingons and the Romulans are still here, and they may not have better things to do than play his games. Suppose further that one of them solves Enowil's problem; he then promises to give them whatever they wish."

Kirk straightened in his chair and gazed directly into Metika's face. "Can you imagine what a Klingon—or a Romulan—would ask for? Would you bet the safety of the Federation that it wouldn't be the plans for some revolutionary new weapons system, so far advanced beyond our present capacities that we would be powerless against it? A moment ago you were talking in terms of hundreds of people; suddenly the stakes have jumped more than a billionfold. There are I don't know how many trillions of beings living within the Federation . . ."

"Approximately 12,682,118,000,000," Spock interrupted. "As of the last official census."

Kirk gave an impatient nod. "That's accurate enough for me. Those are the numbers we're dealing with, Metika. If either the Klingons or the Romulans got their hands on an unstoppable weapon, they could cut through the Federation like a phaser beam through soggy cardboard. Do you have any idea how the Klingons or the Romulans treat the subject peoples living under their domination?"

Metika—and everyone else in the room—was silent for a moment, contemplating the full impact of the captain's supposition. The girl licked her lips thoughtfully, then finally said, "That is a frightening thought—but just how likely is it? You yourself said that Enowil is an ethical being. He doesn't want to hurt anyone. He'd know what the results would be if he gave a superweapon to either of those people. Maybe he'd refuse, and insist that they ask for something more peaceful."

"That is difficult to say," Spock said. "He is considerate enough here within his own bubble. But whether he would be so careful of events outside his sphere of influence is another matter."

"All right, then," Metika came back. She was, after all, an experienced debater and sounded as though she were in her proper milieu. "Let's suppose the worst. Suppose Enowil gives one of our enemies a weapon of incalculable destruction. Anything Enowil can do, the other Organians can do, too—and better, because there are more of them. Do you think the Organians would sit idly by and let a war happen? They intervened once before to stop a war with even less destructive potential. They'd surely act to stop this one."

"I have learned that, where intelligent beings are concerned, past behavior is not a certain indication of future actions," Spock said dryly. "Risking so much on the *probable* intervention of the Organians is a desperate gamble indeed. Also, it must be remembered that the Organians intervened between the Federation and the Klingons because Organia is situated between the two powers and they did not wish to have their own peace disturbed. Organia is *not* located between the Federation and the Romulan Empire; should the Romulan captain solve Enowil's problem, it is a debatable point whether the Organians would intervene in the ensuing war or not."

"They'd have to," Metika replied "Once the Romulans finished with the Federation, they'd naturally attack the Klingons next—and Organia would be in the middle again. I think they could be convinced to act early, before more drastic actions were needed later."

"Your naïve faith in the Organians as a *deus ex machina* is very touching," Kirk said. "As a military officer of the Federation, however, I can't afford to be so trusting. I *have* to consider the worst and plan for it. But just for the sake of argument, let's assume that your ideas are correct, that the Organians would react instantly to any threat from weapons developed by Enowil. Let's even assume a step further—that whoever solves Enowil's problem is smart enough to think of that in advance. After all, we were; we shouldn't underestimate them. That still gives them a wide variety of possible choices that would put the Federation at a strategic disadvantage."

Kirk turned to his chief engineer. "Scotty, suppose you could have anything in the universe, no matter how impossible it seemed. You want to be able to use it to get ahead of your rivals, but it can't be any obvious sort of weapon. Is there anything you can think of that would do the trick?"

Scotty gave a small laugh. "Aye, Captain, there are dozens—thousands. A force field capable of protectin' an entire planet from attack; a detection system capable of tellin' friends from enemies thousands of lightyears away; a new kind of space drive that makes warp speeds look like standin' still; a method of buildin' mechanical systems with a hundred percent energy efficiency—even such a wee beastie as a totally frictionless ballbearing could make a hell of a difference."

"Exactly." Kirk's expression was grim now. "And you have to remember the terms of the Organian Peace Treaty. For each disputed planet to be developed, we and the Klingons must demonstrate which side can develop it most efficiently. A miraculous breakthrough in agriculture, or an economical and fast method of terraforming hostile planets, would literally let them outdistance us in the race for new territory. Even if the two sides never come to blows, they can eventually outgain us to the point where they'll have an economic stranglehold over us. The potential for harm to the Federation is limited only by the imagination—and when it comes to underhanded tricks, neither the Romulans nor the Klingons have shown any lack of imagination."

Metika could realize she'd been outpointed on this particular issue, but she was not yet ready to admit defeat. Sidestepping, she moved to attack from a new angle. "All right, even assuming that you're correct on that point, there still is no guarantee that we'll be able to accomplish any good by staying here. Whether we stay or not, the Klingons and the Romulans probably will—their captains will think of the same arguments you did. Enowil has been thinking about this problem for a century and has gotten nowhere. We could be here for a year or two, and still not be any closer to a solution, only to have one of the others come up with the answer. Just because we're here doesn't prevent our enemies from winning anyway. We can be a force for the positive on Epsilon Delta 4, but here there's no guarantee of anything. You'd be passing up a sure thing just on the chance of accomplishing something here—and you could end up losing both. Is the risk worth it?"

Kirk paused, tilting his head slightly as he contemplated her argument. "You made that point well, and it's something I hadn't considered deeply, it's true. This is a gamble, and the stakes are high—but then, I've always been pretty much of the opinion that a starship captain is a professional gambler, anyway; we just hide the facts in our logs by calling our gambles 'calculated risks.'

"But even if we fail, Metika, even if the Klingons or the Romulans solve the problem before we do, we'll still serve a useful purpose here. Just by being here, and by knowing who won, we'll be valuable reporters when we return to the Federation. Even if we don't know what the winner chooses as his reward, we can at least go back to the Federation Council and tell them to expect trouble from a given area. In war, *any* intelligence is valuable; that knowledge alone could save millions, if not billions, of lives. I'm afraid I have to opt for staying here and seeing this thing through."

"But—"

"If I might make a suggestion, Captain," Spock interposed. "Even had we not been kidnaped into this bubble by Enowil, we would still not have reached Epsilon Delta 4 for another two or three days. Therefore, until that time, we are no worse off here than we would have been in the regular universe. It certainly will not hurt us to examine more closely the magnitude of the problem facing Enowil, and to spend the next several days trying to solve it. By that time, we should be able to estimate well enough whether Enowil's problem belongs in that class of problems which is soluble at all, or whether it is hopeless. If the latter turns out to be the case, we can then ask Enowil once again to let us leave, and he will let us go right next to Epsilon Delta 4. We will have lost no time that we were not originally prepared to lose, and we will not have risked the security of the Federation."

Kirk nodded slowly and looked down the length of the table at Metika. "Is that agreeable to you?" he asked the girl.

Metika clearly did not want to give in. Her friends were in danger, and any compromise in trying to rescue them seemed to her like betrayal. At the same time, she was very well aware of the impression she gave other people—a pretty girl of only twenty standard years, very bright but perhaps lacking in maturity. It infuriated her that youth was automatically equated with immaturity, but she knew that it was. Consequently, she often bent over backward to appear reasonable and conciliatory, even though it sometimes hurt her own cause.

"I suppose I have no other choice," she said bitterly.

"That's quite right," Kirk told her. "As captain, I do have the final say. Whenever possible I like to get a consensus on which to base my decisions, but the decision has to be mine. I can't even promise to hold to Mr. Spock's three-day deadline; if the matter isn't settled by then, I'll have to keep my options open."

As Metika's face fell even further, he added hastily, "I will give every consideration to the colony's problem. That is a promise. The thought of abandoning them rips at my heart, the same as it does at yours. But I have an even larger responsibility, and I can't deny that, either."

Kirk looked around the room and saw no other dissenting faces. Even McCoy, for all his humanitarian concerns, realized the potential danger in letting either the Klingons or the Romulans win this game. "Very well, then," the captain concluded, "we'll tell Enowil that we'll join in his puzzle, at least for the time being. We don't know how many of our crewmembers he'll allow to participate in the guessing game. We'd better prepare some basic lists of whom we'd like to include."

By the time Enowil reappeared on the *Enterprise*'s Bridge, Kirk's crew was ready. The captain had assembled what he considered to be his first-string team to work on this problem: himself, Spock, McCoy, Scotty, Lieutenant Uhura, Lieutenant Sulu and Ensign Chekov. He felt that offered a diverse enough base of opinion that they should be able to solve almost any puzzle.

At the last moment, Metika Spyroukis approached him as well. "Would you mind if I also came along?" she asked.

Kirk's eyes narrowed. In view of her opposition to the entire procedure, he was a little suspicious of her motivation. He did not want to be burdened with any negative influences while trying to solve Enowil's problem. "Any particular reason?"

Metika shrugged. "As long as we're committed to this, I'd like to be in on it. Maybe I can help in some way so that we can win faster and be back on our real mission." Her emphasis on the word "real" was slight, but unmistakeable.

Kirk considered her offer. While young, Metika was quite intelligent, and she had the debater's insight into unusual aspects of an argument. That talent could come in most handy when dealing with Enowil. Another brilliant mind along on the party could only help—and particularly, as she said, because she had the best of reasons for trying to solve the problem quickly. "All right," he nodded, and added a little extra smile. "I'll enjoy your company. I haven't seen much of you since I gave you the tour the other day."

Shortly thereafter, Enowil returned to the Bridge. His appearance was startling to those who hadn't seen him before. He hadn't changed his costume any, except that the outfit now seemed to sparkle with a special glow of its own. Kirk informed the gnome of his decision, and Enowil was delighted. Kirk asked him what the procedure was to be.

"We'll all go down to my world, and you can inspect it and make suggestions. If any member of your party is the first to spot what's missing, your group wins. Simple, isn't it?"

"How many people can I take with me?"

"As many as you like. Too many cooks make light work, as they say."

Kirk waved his hand in a gesture to include the party he had chosen. "I think this number will be sufficient. Do you want us to go to our Transporter Room so that—"

But before he could finish speaking, Enowil, he and his entire party had vanished from the Bridge of the *Enterprise.*

9

They emerged in darkness. Not the complete darkness that had existed aboard the *Enterprise* when it first came through the rift into Enowil's bubble; there was some light. It came from above them, the same pearlescent glow that infused this entire private space. It was not nearly bright enough to read by, but it did provide sufficient illumination for the party from the *Enterprise* to make out the shape of the environment about them.

They were standing on a broad, flat plain that stretched limitlessly to undiscernible horizons. The air was cold, but fortunately there was no wind to make the temperature unbearable. There were two other groups of people standing in clusters near them—presumably, parties from the Romulan and Klingon ships. Enowil, in his costume that continued to sparkle, was the only figure who really stood out in this dim light; he was standing at a point roughly equidistant from all the groups, looking mightily pleased with himself. "Here we are, ladies and gentlemen," he said proudly. "Welcome to my world. I apologize if the conditions are a little raw at first; I don't usually require such things myself, and I'm a trifle rusty. Like wine, cheese and mildew, this will improve with age."

"It's easy to see what you need around here," grumbled the Romulan commander as he stood shivering with his men. "You need light and heat. Anybody would be depressed by the constant gloom and eternal twilight here."

"A good opening guess, Commander Probicol," Enowil said, "but far too obvious, I'm afraid. My world has some of the most spectacular sunrises ever witnessed by intelligent beings—sometimes two or three a day, depending on my mood." He abruptly stopped speaking, lay down on the ground and tilted his head so that his ear was pressed against the dirt. "Ah yes, I can hear it starting now. Prepare yourselves; the sunrise should be in just a few moments."

Looking around him, Kirk could see people bracing themselves for what might be an unusual ordeal. Apparently the crews of the other two ships had also witnessed Enowil's eccentricity in action, and were not sure what to expect.

A warm wind suddenly blew across the plain, removing the biting chill that had slowly been seeping into their bodies. The wind carried the slight scent of peppermint and the blare of distant trumpets. The trumpeting grew louder, announcing the beginning of an important event. Over to one side—for convenience, Kirk arbitrarily labeled it "east" in his own mind—the sky was beginning to lighten with the approaching dawn. The pearlescent glow overhead parted as though it were a set of theater curtains, revealing a bright blue sky with scattered clouds. As the curtain vanished completely, the sky overhead was as bright as noonday, as clear as any childhood memories of a favorite afternoon—but the sun still had not made its appearance.

"Where's—" Commander Probicol began, but Enowil quickly hushed him. The trumpet blare was reaching its frantic crescendo now.

Suddenly the sun made its appearance, shooting over the eastern horizon as though fired by a cannon. It arced overhead into the blue sky until it struck a cloud, at which point it caromed off and bounced to another cloud with a soft thud. The sun continued to bank crazily off one cloud after another until it finally came to rest at a point not quite directly overhead. From its present vantage, it shone down its beneficent warmth and golden rays upon the plain and the frankly awestricken spectators.

Kirk had to blink a couple of times as he watched the sun go through its performance, but as he continued to look at it he noticed a peculiarity. Its surface was not uniformly bright, but was covered with a series of darker markings. Squinting against the glare, he read off the black inscription against the golden background: S-P-O-C-K.

"Why does your sun have my first officer's name on it?" he asked Enowil, half dreading the response.

"I told you I was going to give Spock a gold star, captain. Surely you don't think I'd forget anything as important as that."

Chastened, and sorry he'd asked, Kirk could only mumble, "No, I don't suppose you would."

"A . . . unique spectacle," Spock added, choosing his words with exquisite care. That seemed the best policy when dealing with this daft Organian.

Enowil blushed with definite pride. "Thank you, Mr. Spock. Wait till you see the sunset."

The other bystanders had been looking around themselves at the now-revealed landscape. Captain Kolvor, in charge of the Klingon party, was obviously disapproving. "Is this all there is to the wonderful planet you promised? This flat, boring landscape without so much as a rock to mar its monotony? We Klingons like our worlds rugged and challenging. Your problem is obvious—you should have mountains and deserts and oceans and cliffs."

"And forests, and rivers, and lakes, and geysers, and mesas and canyons," Enowil agreed enthusiastically. "Yes, you're much more into the spirit of things, Captain Kolvor. This world has all that and more. I merely brought you here first so that you could see the sunrise without distractions. *Au naturel,* as it were. Nothing is quite as thrilling as the sight of the morning sun springing into action. However, now that we have been thrilled sufficiently we can move on. We have so much time and so little to see."

He paused. "Wait a minute. Strike that. Reverse it. All right, then, excuse me for the abrupt transition —it won't happen often." He clapped his hands—

—and they were all standing on a small carpeted platform high atop a mountain peak. They were crowded tightly together, as the platform was barely large enough to hold all of them. Enowil floated lightly above their heads, seemingly oblivious to their discomfort. "Can't you make the platform a little bigger?" Lieutenant Sulu called to the gnome.

"I'm afraid you'll have to speak up a bit," Enowil said blithely. "I'm a trifle deaf in my left ear." He waved a hand to indicate the expanse around them. "Here is some of the diversity my planet has to offer."

Diversity there was, in abundance. To one side of their mountain was a wide expanse of sea, with a broad, sandy beach and rocks against which the surf crashed like cymbals. The mountain adjacent to theirs was an active volcano, with a tower of black smoke billowing from its cone. The neighboring mountain on their other side was a flat-topped mesa. Immediately below them, on the side opposite that of the ocean, was a deep gorge through which a raging river roared. Beyond the gorge was a densely clustered forest and, further along the bank, a series of geysers —each spewing water of a different color—spouted dozens of meters into the air. Beyond those, a desert stretched to the horizon, broken only by a scenic lake.

"You can't see my splendid abysses from here, of course, since they're under water," Enowil continued. "And I just couldn't seem to squeeze in the tundra, glaciers and tropical rainforest, but I'm sure you get the general idea. And, naturally enough, the planet has four ice caps, one at each of the poles."

Mr. Spock opened his mouth to say something at this point, but Kirk quickly shushed him. It seemed pointless to get technical with Enowil.

Lieutenant Uhura, squeezing through the crowd to look at the surrounding scenery, was the first to comment. "It's breathtaking," she said, "but it's all so quiet and sterile. Except for ourselves and the surf, I don't hear any sounds or see any signs of life. Could that be what you're missing?"

"Dear lady, you are most perceptive, but I'm afraid I also thought of that long ago. This world is supplied with a veritable plethora—if, indeed, there is any other kind of plethora—of animal and plant life. If I may be permitted to demonstrate . . . ?"

He twirled his hand dramatically three times, and the platform upon which they stood began to move. Like a tobaggan, it tilted to one side and began gliding rapidly down the mountainside. The passengers on the crowded platform clung to one another instinctively, regardless of their various races, as the platform careened downward at breakneck speed. Overhead, Enowil kept pace with them, the wind ruffling his curly hair and whipping the point of his cap around his head. "They must downward still, and onward, who would keep abreast of Truth," he cried with gleeful intensity.

Though the angle of descent was steep and their speed was dizzying, the ride at least was smooth and free of bumps. When the platform reached the bottom of the mountainside it abruptly leveled off, tossing everyone backward into the person behind him. The journey was far from over, however, as the platform only accelerated and continued rushing straight ahead.

"How much further do we have to go like this?" the Klingon captain called.

"Half a league, half a league, half a league onward," Enowil replied cheerily.

The platform swooped through the forest, darting in and out among the trees and missing some of them by the meagerest of margins. It was considerably more than half a league, by Kirk's reckoning, before the platform pulled to an abrupt stop in front of an enormous white marble gateway. "All ashore that's going ashore," Enowil called, and the passengers needed no second invitation. They left the platform as though it were a burning building.

As they gathered together in groups before the gate, they were not quite as distant from one another as they'd been previously. The different races had had to crowd together on the platform and cling to one another for support; it was hard, for the moment, to remember that they were implacable enemies.

"Exhilarating, wasn't it?" Enowil said. "Welcome to my little menagerie. I have in here representative samples of the kinds of animals that inhabit my world. It's not complete by a long shot, but if you think anything is missing, let me know."

"What about that?" Romulan Commander Probicol pointed to a sign that was suspended over the archway leading through the gates into the menagerie. The sign read: ABANDON HOPE, ALL YE WHO ENTER HERE.

Enowil looked up and scowled. "Oh, that. Careless of me. Left over from a previous existence, undoubtedly; I have to re-use props sometimes, you know. How's this?" The lettering of the sign suddenly changed, so that now it read: METROPOLIS CITY ZOO. He clapped his hands. "Now, onward. There is still so much to see."

The entourage followed Enowil on foot through the gates into the zoo. They were rapidly ceasing to be amazed at mere size, and the fact that the gates towered nearly three stories above their heads failed to impress them. If Enowil was disappointed by their lack of reaction, though, he didn't show it; the beings he was about to exhibit would more than make up for it.

The path was paved with a firm yet resilient material halfway between cement and hard rubber; it had a pleasant feel to it as it meandered through the bushes and shrubberies until it came, at last, to a cleared area where they saw their first animals. It was a small pack of canine-looking creatures whose skins were blazing with light. The creatures seemed to be suffering no pain, although they were flaming brightly. One of them looked up as the group approached and trotted over in a friendly manner.

"Look out!" one of the Klingons cried, fearing the burning creature would come too close and endanger them all.

Enowil raised a hand calmly. "No need to worry, sir. We are adequately protected."

Lieutenant Sulu, looking closely, observed, "They're locked up in a cage of glass, so we can see in without bars or obstructions."

"Glass walls do not a prism make," Enowil nodded.

"But what are those things?" Uhura asked.

"Those, my dear lady, are firedogs. They belong to the same family as other fire creatures—fireflies, firedrakes and the like. A most incendiary bunch. But step lively, these are just the beginnings of the wonders I have to show you." He redoubled his pace and led them along the path through the brush until the firedogs were lost to view.

On their left, they passed a grove of trees with most unusual fruit. On the branches grew footwear of all descriptions—everything from baby booties and sandals, through pumps and penny loafers, all the way to mukluks and galoshes. Dr. McCoy nudged Kirk in the ribs. "A shoetree, no doubt."

"Quiet, Bones, you'll only encourage him."

Enowil apparently did not hear either of them, for he continued his spiel without hesitation. "Up ahead we have probably the most unusual and certainly the most pampered of all my creatures." He pointed to another glass cage wherein an enormous, fat *thing* squatted. This animal was larger than a hippopotamus, with mounds of blubber weighing it down. Its hairless skin was lavender, mottled with large splotches of darker purple. Though it seemed to be basically a quadruped, its bulk was so enormous that it would have had difficulty moving anywhere. As the group approached its cage, the creature opened one eye lazily to examine them, then closed it and went back to sleep.

"This," Enowil continued proudly, "is a creature you've all heard of: the famous Time Being whom everyone is always doing things for."

The Romulan commander snorted. "I doubt that."

Enowil looked at him closely. "Oh, my dear Commander Probicol, you must never, never doubt what nobody knows. The Time Being is, of course, closely related to that other fabulous creature, the Nonce. I'd show you him, too, but the two are so similar that it would be almost a redundancy, and there are so many more of my wonderful animals to be seen— the prairie oysters, the meniscus, the delightful copycat who's better than any chameleon . . ."

"I think," Kirk said, "we're all willing to concede that you have indeed created a masterful assortment of unique animals. It might be more profitable if we moved on to something else."

Enowil's face fell, and he looked like a little boy whose promised trip to the candy store had been canceled. "But Captain Kirk, there's so much I wanted to show you, so many wonders that will have you gasping in amazement. . . ."

"I'm sure there are, but if we're here to solve your problem our time can better be spent somewhere there's a lack rather than someplace where, as you yourself admit, you have plenty of a given item."

Enowil regained his composure, squared his shoulders and looked up at Kirk. "You're absolutely right. I'm being incredibly selfish, and that is not the mark of a good host. Please forgive me. I do have one creation, though, that I must insist on showing you before we move on. Since it was the lovely lady over here," and he bowed in Uhura's direction, "who made the suggestion of animals, I have one especially for her. It is from Africa, in tribute to the land of her heritage."

As he spoke, an enormous male lion trotted out of the bushes, his sleek, tawny body in the peak of condition. Seeing the group, he gave a low growl and started padding directly toward Uhura—slowly at first, but he picked up speed as he neared until he was moving at a full charge.

The communications officer screamed as the large cat came bounding at her. Kirk, seeing the danger, instinctively leaped to her defense. As the lion sprang at her, Kirk interposed his body between the animal and Uhura, taking the full brunt of the beast's charge as it crashed into him. Kirk was knocked to the ground by the heavy creature and threw up an arm to protect his face and eyes from the raking claws he expected at any second.

Instead he was nearly deafened by a low rumbling sound that he realized belatedly was the lion's purr. A large rough tongue rasped along his forearm as the huge beast licked him in a friendly manner.

Enowil stood over the pair on the ground, looking down with vast bemusement. "And darest thou, then," he asked, "to beard the lion in his den, the Douglas in his hall? You are a man of rare courage, Captain Kirk, though of less-than-average memory. I told you nothing here would be harmful; did you forget so soon? I merely wanted to create a tribute to your lovely officer."

"When I want a tribute, I'll ask for it," Uhura said, impressed by her captain's bravery in her defense and upset with the gnome for mocking him. "And I prefer my animals a little more soft and cuddly, thank you."

Enowil was taken aback by the sudden outburst, and stared down at his feet dejectedly. "I'm sorry," he said. "I only intended to please you. I hadn't realized you would be this fussy."

He pulled the lion away from Kirk, spanked it and sent it loping off down the path in the opposite direction. Kirk stood up slowly, dusting himself off and eyeing his host with suspicion. Enowil was pouting like a child, and that was a dangerous emotional state for anyone as powerful as he was. Kirk was wondering whether the mad Organian would choose to banish them from further competition out of displeasure.

Enowil, though, after a moment of silence, regained most of his customary ebullience. "Well, be that as it may, there are further things to see and we can't dwell forever on our failures. Would anyone else care to hazard a guess as to what my world is lacking?"

10

McCoy leaned over to whisper in Kirk's ear. "What this world lacks most," he said, "is a sense of perspective and consistent standards on the part of its manager."

Enowil's sharp ears, however, had picked up the doctor's comment. The Organian turned to McCoy and clucked his tongue accusingly. "What a dreadful passion is that pride, which would force men to think like ourselves!" he said. "I heard that remark, Doctor, and it's not really germane to the issue at hand. It took me millennia, by your paltry standards, to develop my personality, and I'm quite satisfied with it. It is my immediate surroundings that I seek to change. Very few beings are ever blessed with that option, and I wish to take advantage of it. Kindly direct your attentions to the kind of environment that best suits my personality—short, of course, of a straitjacket and rubber room. I'd find those most tedious."

"It seems to me," said one Romulan, "that this world of yours must be very lonely. Aside from yourself and some animals and plants, and a very muddled geological structure, there's no one to talk to. I think that is why you've really called us here—you wanted some company."

"Ah, yes. Good company and good discourse are

the very sinews of virtue," Enowil replied. "I assure you, my world does not lack for inhabitants. You haven't seen any yet because it's still early; the sun just rose a little while ago, you'll recall. I brought you to my glass menagerie before the official opening time, so that you could look about at the animals without distraction; I sense, however, that the gates are now opening to the general public, so I would suggest that we all step to one side and keep together to avoid becoming lost in the throngs."

He motioned everyone into a small clearing beside the main path and began looking back toward the entrance. At first nothing was apparent. Then a young woman came along, holding the hands of her two little children. She was busy talking to them and pointing out various things as they walked, but she took the time to smile at Enowil and the others as she passed them and continued deeper into the zoo.

No one else appeared for a moment, and Kirk began to wonder whether that was the extent of this world's population. Then more people appeared walking along the pathway, small knots of them at first, but in a very short time the clumps began to coalesce into a mob as more and more beings crowded their way into the zoo. There were members of every race in the Galaxy that Kirk had ever seen, plus a sizeable number that he hadn't. Tall, short, fat, thin, winged, finned, biped, triped, quadruped. Some were covered with hair, or scales, or feathers, or fur, while others were completely bald. Their skins were in every hue of the rainbow, and some of them even changed color as Kirk watched. The body odors of so many different races mingled like the midnight shift at a perfumery, and the increasing volume of their random conversations became a pounding wave of surf against rocks.

The groups from the three ships drew more tightly together as the crowd surged around them, an ever-increasing number. The atmosphere was becoming claustrophobic, even in this open park, as more and more people, people without limit, entered the zoo.

Now they were shoved so tightly together that they could barely move, each person's shoulders touching those of his neighbor—but none of the newcomers seemed to feel there was anything unusual in this. They continued their conversations with their friends, even as more people pushed their way onto the path. If this were to keep up, it would become impossible to move at all, and everyone would merely be pressed up against the next until the life was eventually squeezed out of him.

"You see," Enowil said to the Romulan who'd made the suggestion, "people are no problem at all. I can have all the company I want."

"This is not precisely what I had in mind," the Romulan continued stubbornly. "I meant people with whom you could talk and discuss matters, and possibly even argue." He was having to yell to make himself heard above the din of the crowd that was pressing in on all sides. "Sheer numbers of people is not enough to do any good."

"People, people everywhere, nor any stop to think, eh? You're quite right, the madding crowd can become oppressive at times. Fortunately I do have other recourse. Follow me."

"How?" Kolvor, the Klingon captain, asked sarcastically. "We'll never get through that crushing mass of bodies. It's impossible."

"The man who claims something is impossible is invariably right, for *he* will never do it," Enowil said. "Of course we can't go out that way. We'll take the sky-bridge instead."

Kolvor's next question, "What sky-bridge?" died on his lips as a golden arch appeared in front of Enowil, curving high up into the sky for what appeared to be many kilometers, only to descend to earth again far off into the distance. The surface of the bridge was a rapidly moving walkway, and there were railings on either side of the bridge to keep anyone from falling off. Without waiting for further discussion Enowil stepped onto the bridge and the walkway quickly carried him up and out of sight. "Swifter than centaurs after rapine bent," he exclaimed as he disappeared.

The rest of the group, not wishing to be left behind, hurriedly followed his example. They had to climb onto the bridge single file because it was so narrow, and they jammed together at the entrance attempting to get on all at once. There was no order to the boarding and by the time Kirk got on, he found himself standing next to Captain Kolvor. The moving walkway under their feet carried them rapidly into the air, arching over the crowded menagerie.

Kolvor looked at Kirk and gave him a sardonic smile. "Frustrating, isn't it?" he asked.

"In what way?" Kirk was by nature suspicious of all Klingons; he'd had too many dealings with them to be anything else.

"In *all* ways. Dealing with a madman is most exasperating. As I'm sure you know, we Klingons prefer direct action to guessing games like these."

Kirk shrugged his shoulders. "Enowil's in charge around here, and he sets the rules." He smiled back at Kolvor. "You could always drop out if you get too frustrated."

"I think not." Kolvor's expression never wavered. "Forfeiture is not the Klingon way. I was thinking more along the lines of a partnership between us, thereby doubling our chances against the Romulans."

"I thought you and the Romulans were allies. Are you willing to betray them for us?"

"'Betray' is such an unfair word. The Romulan and Klingon empires have a mutual trade agreement, nothing more. We owe no loyalty to them, nor they to us. There is nothing to prevent you and me from coming to a separate agreement concerning this contest."

"I see." Kirk steadied himself momentarily on the railing as the walkway reached the top of the arch and began curving downward again. "And exactly what sort of agreement did you have in mind?"

The Klingon bent his head closer to Kirk's, lowered

his voice and became even more conspiratorial. "If the Romulans were not around, it would significantly enhance our own chances of winning, would it not?"

"Do you really think we could talk them out of competition?"

The Klingon gave a mirthless snort. "That is the major difference between us, Captain. You people of the Federation think of talk; we Klingons think of more direct action. Consider for a moment—a well-placed bomb aboard the Romulan vessel would destroy not only it, but their chances of effectively competing against us as well."

Kirk could well believe that. He could also well believe that Kolvor would first have approached the Romulans with a similar offer against the *Enterprise;* whether the pact between those two powers was as loose as Kolvor described or not, they made natural allies against the Federation. The fact that Kolvor was now offering Kirk a deal probably meant that the Romulans had turned him down. That made sense to Kirk, in a way; he knew that the Romulans, while ferocious antagonists, nevertheless maintained a rigid code of honor—something the Klingons themselves lacked completely. The Romulans would not consider it honorable to win in such a fashion—and neither did Kirk.

"I'm afraid I'll have to turn you down on this deal," he said. "Enowil might not take too kindly to us if he found we were cheating." Kirk's eyes narrowed. "Of course, if you really don't think you're smart enough to solve the puzzle on your own . . ."

Kolvor snorted. "Even a Klingon imbecile can match wits with the best either the Romulans or the Federation has to offer."

"Then you're really at no disadvantage as things currently stand, are you?" Kirk smiled at the other captain, all sweetness and light. Another reason for his refusal, which he was diplomatic enough not to give aloud, was that he could almost count on treachery from the Klingon if he agreed to the deal.

If Kolvor was willing to betray the Romulans, his erstwhile allies, he would be equally willing to betray the Federation.

Before the Klingon had a chance to reply, their ride on the sky-bridge came to an abrupt end as the moving walkway deposited them on a paved sidewalk before a large red brick building. An arch of white stone over the doorway proclaimed, in golden letters, "The Forum." There was a smaller sign beside the door that said simply, "Spats Encouraged."

Kirk had to step quickly to the side as more people emerged from the bridge behind him. Enowil was standing at the top of the short flight of steps next to the door, looking out over the increasing group below him and tapping his foot with impatience. "Hurry, hurry," he cried, despite the fact that those still on the bridge could not come any faster than they were already moving. "Mustn't dawdle, mustn't dawdle."

Finally, when they were all assembled before him once more, he said, "For those of you who find life too agreeable here, may I present the Forum, a debating society. As the founding member, I invite you all in as my guests—but I warn you, hold very tightly to your own opinions. Sweet reason has a tendency to curdle in here."

The doors opened and the group filed inside. They found a long hallway with large, well-appointed rooms branching off to either side at intervals. The rooms were wood-paneled and carpeted with plush velvet fabrics. Padded leather easy chairs were scattered about the rooms, while crystal chandeliers dangled from the ceilings and illuminated the chambers. Each room was two stories tall and lined almost completely with bookshelves. The principal ornamentation, though, was the profusion of clocks that were ubiquitous throughout the club. From tall, stately grandfather clocks to small mantelpiece clocks, there was at least one timepiece no matter where one looked—and each clock displayed a different time. It was as though no one could agree on so simple a thing as what time it was. But, considering the nature of the sunrise, time could not be a simple phenomenon on this planet.

In the rooms, also, were the society's members, beings of all known races gathered here for the sole purpose of airing their differences. There was a constant buzzing of conversation throughout the building that, at times of excessive acrimony, threatened to become a roar.

The general pandemonium within the building made it impossible to hear everything that was going on. Kirk turned his primary attention to an argument over in one corner where a tall, blue-skinned Andorian was arguing furiously with a pudgy, multilimbed Rafellian.

"But surely you must realize that free will must be restrained to avoid undue impetuosity," the Andorian was saying. He was so emotional that his antennae were actually twitching—a phenomenon Kirk had never seen before. "It does not require a surrender to determinism to realize that the quantum mechanical randomness guarantees the variability of reality despite any ordered impositions of scientific principles to the contrary."

"Mere obfuscation," the Rafellian snorted. "You have obviously abandoned the argument of responsibility to the metaphysical ethos. The Heisenberg Principle clearly demonstrates the *calculability* of the uncertainties to which you so glibly allude. It is my contention that sheer indeterminate quantities do not in and of themselves constitute a graphic example of universal metavariance—nor even, to put it more bluntly, of isolated variant pockets within a metastable system."

Kirk shook his head. The arguments, for all their impressive sound, seemed to him just one hair the other side of sanity. There was the feeling that he might understand them if he strained just a little more—but along with that feeling was the fear that such straining would take him beyond the bounds of reason.

The Andorian paused for a moment to digest his adversary's remarks and weigh his response. "Apparently the insolubility of the general equations for the n-body problem is just some local triviality, I presume. Can you honestly maintain that the metamorphosis of entropy is so conveniently disdained—or worse, inherently refutable? So facile a hypothesis is not consistent with an empirical overview."

"Pinbrain!" snarled the Rafellian.

"Bubbleface!" the Andorian retorted.

Almost simultaneously, the two antagonists launched themselves at one another, falling to the floor and rolling around in tight wrestling grips. The Andorian had a size advantage, but the Rafellian had more arms to use, and was much more difficult to contain. Their violent thrashings knocked over tables and pushed chairs about the room, but none of the other members of the debating society took any notice of them.

Kirk looked to Enowil. "Aren't you going to do anything about them?"

Enowil peered casually in the direction of the two combatants. "An argument needs no reason, nor a friendship," he proclaimed calmly, and strolled off in another direction.

Kirk and the others saw similar scenes repeated as they wandered haphazardly through the building. Arguments might begin on an exalted and rarified plane, but all too frequently they broke down into physical aggression. Sometimes, in the larger debates, as many as ten people might be involved, and the ensuing fracas had as much decorum as a barroom brawl.

Metika Spyroukis, a trained debater, took her arguments seriously—and what she saw about her raised her anger to a white-hot fury. "This is no debating society," she railed at Enowil. "It's a lunatic asylum for inmates who've swallowed dictionaries."

Enowil cocked his head and stared straight into her eyes. There was a look of benign innocence on his face. "You really must learn to enunciate more distinctly," he said. "Try pronouncing the syllables one at a time if you wish to be understood." Then he turned away to give his attention to some other matter.

Her anger raging unchecked, Metika stomped back to where Kirk was standing. "This whole thing is impossible," she said, waving her arms vehemently. "We're not going to find any answer, nobody is. This madman is just playing games with us. Look how much amusement he's getting from all this, grinning from ear to ear like a Cheshire cat. It doesn't matter whether what we mention has existed before on this world or not; all he has to do is *say* it did, and we're forced to take his word for it. He's turning all of this into a vast circus, and *we're* the clowns."

"Calm down, Metika," Kirk soothed. "What would you suggest we do?"

"We can leave, as I asked before. At least we could accomplish something positive on Epsilon Delta 4. You don't have to worry about the Romulans or the Klingons getting any superweapons—no one's going to win anything here. Enowil's insane, and he's just toying with us."

The captain considered her request. While to all intents and purposes her appraisal of Enowil's sanity seemed correct, Kirk thought he detected a false ring to it—as though Enowil, like Hamlet, was "but mad north-northwest." If he waited for the right southerly wind, something might yet come of this adventure.

"Let's hold on a little while longer," he said. "As Mr. Spock said, we weren't expecting to arrive at the colony for another day or so, anyway. Have patience for at least that long, and then we'll re-evaluate."

Metika harrumphed and stormed off. It was obvious that her patience was exhausted.

From his position a few meters away, Captain

Kolvor could not help overhearing the exchange between Kirk and the girl. *Perhaps something can be made of this,* he smiled—and a Klingon's smile is a sinister expression.

11

While Captain Kirk was occupied with Metika, and while the mayhem within the Forum was raging unabated, Mr. Spock approached Enowil. The gnome looked up at the tall Vulcan. "Well, Mr. Spock, what do you think?"

"I think," Spock said slowly, "that there is enough dissension in this one building to satisfy even the creature our ship once encountered that thrived on other people's fights. But dissension alone will not provide the proper intellectual stimulation that a being of your advanced development requires. It is my contention that what you're lacking here is not argument per se but intellectual stimulation—a challenge to the powerful, driving mind you obviously possess."

"That sounds like you're trying to flatter me, Mr. Spock."

"I assure you, Enowil, that a Vulcan would never stoop to flattery."

"Oh, I know that. And it also can't be flattery since it's perfectly true. Unfortunately, your hypothesis is one that also occurred to me, quite some time ago." He raised his voice now, so that the rest of the party could hear as well. "Mr. Spock has suggested that I lack mental stimulation. The answer to his challenge, by strange coincidence, is in the basement of this very building. If you would all be so kind as to follow me?"

They were all delighted to leave the debating society to its own arguments. Kirk, for one, was starting to get a headache from the combination of noise and indefinable logic.

Enowil led them all to an enormous elevator car. "I think this should be large enough for all of us," he said and, to no one's surprise, he turned out to be right. When everyone was inside, the elevator doors slid silently shut before them and Enowil pressed the large button on the control panel marked "B." With a jerk, the elevator started moving.

"I thought you said we were going to the basement," one of the Romulans said.

"And so we are," Enowil answered. "Quite observant of you, my good fellow."

"But the elevator is going up."

"What goes up must come down, mustn't it? Providing, of course, it has not reached the escape velocity for the planet of given mass. And anyway, I have been known to keep my basements in strange places. Ah, here we are: Intellectual Stimulation. All out, please."

The travelers left the elevator and found themselves in an immense darkened room, illuminated only by the light from large electronic scoreboards on the walls overhead. Each board was at least twenty meters by ten in size, and covered with thousands of tiny squares, some of which were lit by lights of various colors. "Behold, Mr. Spock," Enowil said, "a game of fascinating complexity. Each square you see on the board contains a number—positive or negative, integral or fractional, rational or irrational, real or imaginary. You play against the computer, which has been specifically designed to select its squares at random so that you—or I, for that matter—cannot predict in advance which squares it will play. You pick a certain number of squares, depending on which turn it is; on your first turn you pick one square, on the second you pick two, on the third three, and so forth. On the computer's first turn it picks one, on its second four, on its third nine, and so forth. You keep picking, alternating turns with the machine, until the entire board has been lit up.

"The object of the game is that the numbers you pick must establish a given pattern—for instance, to give a simplistic example, all the numbers you pick during a given turn should add to an even positive integer. The machine, of course, acting at random, will tend to foul up your subsequent turns, since once a square is lit the other player can't use it. As I said, that was a simplistic example; when I myself play, I prefer a more challenging requirement—perhaps that the sum of the numbers I pick be a perfect square or that the sum of the numbers I pick, when divided by the number of the turn, turns out to be a prime number. The number of variations is limited only by my imagination—and fortunately I haven't reached the end of that yet. Would you care to try a game, Mr. Spock?"

"By all means," the Vulcan said. "It sounds fascinating."

"Let's make it easy for your first try, shall we? All the numbers within the squares will be positive integers, and the sum of the numbers at the end of each turn must be a multiple of thirteen. Have fun."

As Spock stepped into the center of the darkened room and began addressing the computer, nearly all eyes were on him. To Kolvor, this diversion offered a unique opportunity. The Klingon captain, as was typical of his race, had been looking for some method of gaining an advantage over the other two groups in this bizarre contest. His attempts at fueling the enmity between the Federation and the Romulan teams had been thwarted when both captains proved to be too honorable to attempt to sabotage the other one. He had thus been forced to step back, temporarily, and await whatever chance fate might throw him. He had not had to wait very long.

Sidling casually up to Metika, he said, "May I have a word with you, my lady?"

"I don't think we have much in common," she answered coldly.

"Perhaps not, perhaps a great deal. We both want this farce to be ended as quickly as possible, don't we? Would you just allow me to explain my position?"

"I don't seem able to stop you."

Kolvor looked around to make sure no one—particularly not Kirk—was watching him, and lowered his voice still further. "We Klingons do not want to participate in this insane game Enowil is playing. Our ship was on its way home after a long extended mission, and our people are homesick. We don't really think there is anything to be gained by staying here. We would much rather be about our own business."

"Then why don't you leave? Enowil won't keep you here against your will."

"Ah, but there's the problem. We don't dare leave—not as long as the Romulans and your own party are here—because there is always the *chance* that Enowil actually may give what he has promised to one of the others. As a military man, that's a chance I simply can't take."

Metika gave a sardonic laugh. "Yes, that's the only thing keeping us here, too. We have to perform an emergency evacuation of an endangered colony, yet we're stuck here because Captain Kirk doesn't trust you or the Romulans."

"I thought as much. You and I both want to leave, but mutual distrust keeps us here against our wills. What a shame we can't break down those barriers. Trust must begin someplace, you know. If only it could begin here, with us, who can tell where it might lead?"

Kolvor could tell that the girl was weakening slightly in her resistance to him, but she tried hard not to show it. "That's all very noble," she said, "but what about the Romulans? In a situation like this, the trust has to work three ways, not just two."

"Ah yes, the Romulans." Kolvor stroked his goatee thoughtfully. "They are indeed a problem. I have already brought the matter up with Commander Probicol, and his response was most disheartening. It seems that his ship was merely on a routine patrol, and had no urgent business to perform. There is no pressure on him—he could stay here for weeks or even months, without any worries. He can afford to take the long gamble, where you and I cannot. He has already told me that he plans to stay here as long as is necessary. Perhaps he hopes to wait us out."

"Then there's little point in our establishing a mutual trust, is there? As long as the Romulans are prepared to wait, you'll have to stay here—and so, probably, will we." Her pretty face screwed up into a sour expression as she realized that Captain Kirk would never leave here as long as there was a chance the other groups might win.

"But what if a solution could be found? Would you be willing to help implement it for our mutual benefit?"

"You're talking as though you already have something in mind."

Kolvor gave her a smile. "I can see there's no use trying to fool you. Yes, I do have a plan, and I would like your help. The Romulans are refusing to quit the game *voluntarily*, but it may be possible to force them to leave."

"Now you're starting to sound like a Klingon."

"You don't mean that as a compliment, I'm sure, but I'll ignore it. My thought was that if the Romulan ship were destroyed, the Romulans would have to pull out of the competition."

"That's a big if. As I recall, you tried to attack our ship when we first appeared, and Enowil changed your photon torpedo into harmless fireworks. What makes you think he'll let you destroy the Romulans?"

"I now realize my mistake. A photon torpedo is too obvious; it can be detected and intercepted from the instant it's launched until the instant it reaches its target. A bomb is another matter. It's very secretive; if you place it right, no one even knows it's there until it goes off. A single charge, planted at the baffle between the matter and antimatter chambers, is all it would take; the ship would be blown to a powder."

"You said you needed my help," Metika said suspiciously. "Where do I fit into all of this?"

"I need you to plant the bomb."

Metika shook her head vigorously. "Oh, no. Why should I do your dirty work? Why can't you have one of your own people do it?"

The Klingon captain pretended to look hurt. "It again boils down to a question of trust. If we are to trust each other's motives and dedication, we must operate in this venture together. How am I to know that you really want to leave? Maybe you just want me to destroy the Romulans myself and then go, while you pretend to go and actually stay here. I need some assurance that you are as eager to leave as we are—and what better proof than your helping us blow up the Romulan ship, thus accomplishing our mutual goal?"

"But why should I be the one to plant the bomb?"

"I'm supplying the idea; I'll even supply the bomb. You have to provide *something*."

Metika thought carefully, realizing that she was approaching the biggest decision of her young life. "It would be murder," she said slowly. "There are still some people aboard that ship."

"I was of the impression that they were your enemies."

"Yes, they've attacked Federation planets lots of times without warning, killing innocent men and women. But there is technically a truce now; I could be responsible for starting another war."

"No war will start over this," Kolvor assured her. "Even if they were to learn who planted the bomb —and I certainly have no intention of telling them— the Romulans would not go to war over an incident like this. They can no more afford a war than can the Federation or the Klingon Empire. It would take a much more serious provocation, believe me."

"But still—I've never killed anyone before."

"The *Talon* is a small ship," Kolvor continued. "Judging from the size of the party Commander Probicol brought down here with him, there can't be more than ten or twenty people left on board. How many people are on that colony world that must be evacuated?"

"Six hundred and eighty," Metika said. Her voice was barely more than a whisper.

"I'll leave it to you, then. Compare six hundred and eighty lives against ten. Granted, you Federation people are much softer about killing than we Klingons are—but the choice seems simple to me. A greater evil versus a lesser one—that's what you must decide."

Metika closed her eyes tightly and bowed her head. "I—I'll have to talk it over with Captain Kirk."

"No," Kolvor said firmly. He could clearly see that he had her soul now—she wanted very much for her conscience to permit her to do what he asked—and he dared not allow Kirk to talk her out of it . . . which the Federation captain was certain to do. "I've already talked to him, and he wants nothing to do with it. He refused to trust me; he said he'd rather sacrifice the entire colony than take a chance on a Klingon."

Metika raised her head once more and opened her eyes. There was a hard glint in them that Kolvor approved of. "He would," she said bitterly.

At this moment their conversation was interrupted by the sound of applause. Spock had finished playing his game with the computer, and had managed to "win"—that is, the sum of the numbers in the squares he picked during each round were always multiples of thirteen. Enowil was the first to offer congratulations. "You did a magnificent job for a beginner," he said enthusiastically. "Of course, this was a simplified version—and I normally play four or more boards simultaneously, with a different game on each. But will you concede that there is enough intellectual stimulation here to last me for a while?"

"Indeed there is. The randomness of your computer insures that no two games will ever be alike."

"And this is only one of the games I've invented," Enowil said with pride. "If you'd like to see some of the others . . ."

"This has been sufficient. I will concede that your world does not lack for challenges to your mind."

Once again Enowil appeared slightly disappointed that he could not show off his creations further, but he was resolved to hide the feeling more bravely. "Does anyone else have any more suggestions at this time?"

Dr. McCoy cleared his throat. "This is all very nice," he said hesitantly, "and I know there may be some error in judging your needs by my own—but I've spotted one missing item so far that would drive me personally 'round the bend. May I speak bluntly?"

"Of course," Enowil said. "We're all mature adults here."

McCoy held up a hand and began ticking points off on his fingers. "First, you don't lack for company; there are more than enough people to suit anyone's tastes. Second, you have people you can talk to and argue with, and even these computers to play games. Maybe it's just the plain country doctor in me, or maybe it's the dirty old man, but I don't sense the combination of emotional and physical release that . . . oh, damn it, why don't I just say it? What about sex?"

A wicked grin spread slowly across Enowil's face. "The old *cherchez la femme*, eh, Doctor? Surely you were told that we Organians forsook our corporeal bodies centuries ago in favor of more intellectual pursuits. Do you really think I would need something so vulgar?"

"Well, speaking as a doctor . . ."

"You're absolutely right. My fellow Organians would never admit it, of course, but even in the form of pure energy there are certain—'activities'—which could be construed as our own analogs of the sexual experience. In other words, we get it on just like you mortals. The form, of course, is quite different from anything you could possibly understand, but perhaps . . ."

Enowil fell silent for a moment as he pondered the problem. Then a smile lit up his visage. "Yes, that's it. I can translate it all for you in terms that you couldn't possibly misunderstand. Oh, this is exciting! Follow me, all of you." And he raced out of the room before any of the others could voice reservations or objections to this new development. Reluctantly, the three parties could only follow their host and hope for the best.

Kolvor grabbed Metika by the elbow. "Well, are you with me or not? You must decide now."

Metika tried to speak, but words refused to come. Feeling a queasiness in the pit of her stomach, she could only nod her agreement.

Inwardly, Captain Kolvor was bursting with triumph. He would have this foolish Federation girl blow up the Romulan ship for him, and then he would denounce the whole affair as a Federation plot. The Romulans would be destroyed and the *Enterprise* would likely be banished for not playing fair, leaving the Klingons as the only possible winners in this crazy game. The Klingon leader was already contemplating the honors in store for him when his ship returned home with the prize—whatever he chose it to be—won from the mad Organian.

Or perhaps he should not return home with it at all. If he used his imagination well enough, he could wind up with a weapon so powerful that he, Kolvor, could conquer the Federation, the Romulan Empire, and the Klingon Empire as well, and he would rule as the supreme power in the entire Galaxy. The thought was a warming one.

He forced himself to cut short that line of speculation. Everything must be dealt with in its own time. "We must leave now," he told the girl. "It will be a while before they miss us—and by then it will be too late."

He used his pocket communicator to call his ship, and a few moments later both he and Metika were quietly beamed up to the Klingon vessel.

12

Less than an hour later, Metika Spyroukis materialized near the engine room of the Romulan ship *Talon*. She had her phaser drawn, ready for trouble in case she appeared where any of the crew could see her, but she was in luck—the corridor was empty save for herself. Tucking her weapon back into its holster, she bent down to lift the bomb that had materialized on the floor beside her.

The bomb was essentially a large box with a set of dials on one side. It was so large it filled both her arms as she carried it; she could only hope her luck would hold out for another few minutes so that she could get it properly placed. If she ran into any Romulans now, she'd be dead. Fortunately, the bomb was lighter than it looked, and she was able to move rapidly down the halls toward her destination.

Because the Klingons and the Romulans used similar types of ships, Kolvor had been able to give her a brief orientation to direct her toward the crucial area. Normally the process could be simplified by beaming her directly to the spot she wanted—but when dealing with the juncture between the matter and antimatter chambers, even the tiniest error in placement could have dire consequences. Kolvor and Metika both agreed it would be safer to transport her

116

to a point *near* the baffle and let her walk the rest of the way.

Though she was in a hurry, she could not help but notice the walls of the corridor around her. Like most citizens of the Federation, she had an image of the Romulans as being spartan in their tastes, but she actually found this decor rather pleasing. The walls were covered with a special plastic material that gave the appearance of polished marble, and along the top, like a molding, was a string of friezes depicting miniature figures engaged in acts of combat and hero-ism. It gave her the impression of being within a large, official building rather than a cold, impersonal spaceship.

Her footsteps sounded terribly loud to her own ears as she moved hastily down the hallway, but there was still no sign of anyone else. Not only did that make her feel safer, but it eased her conscience as well—perhaps the entire crew was down on Enowil's planet and she would only be blowing up an empty ship, after all. She didn't really believe that, but it was comforting to contemplate a case where no one would die from her actions.

She reached the door Kolvor had told her to expect, the one that led into the power room. There were signs on the door and on the walls to either side of it, all written in the strange characters of the Romulan language which Metika neither recognized nor under-stood. She assumed they were warnings that the area was off-limits to all but authorized personnel, but she was not about to let that stop her.

As she and Kolvor had assumed, the door did not automatically slide open when she approached it. Setting her bomb gently down beside the door for a moment, she reached into her pocket and pulled out the special sonic key the Klingon captain had given her. She aimed it at the door and pressed the tiny stud on the side and, as Kolvor had promised, the power room door slid invitingly ajar.

Metika gave the inside of the room a quick scan,

but there was still no one in sight. Picking up her package once again, she carried it into the almost-bare room beyond the doorway. There were banks of meters lining one wall; a control panel beneath them contained multiple rows of dials and switches. One solitary chair, empty at present, stood before the controls. The rest of the room was devoid of furnishing except for a large square hole in the far wall. The hole led into a tunnel that was dimly lit with red light; it was that tunnel which separated the matter and antimatter chambers that powered this ship. Kolvor had warned her that it would be certain death to venture inside that tunnel without a protective suit, but fortunately Metika did not have to go inside; she merely had to set the timer on the bomb and push it through the mouth of the tunnel. The bomb would take care of itself from then on.

She walked over to the tunnel entrance and set her box down once more, making sure it was on its side with the controls facing upward. Kolvor had given her a quick course in how to set the bomb and, though her fingers were shaking slightly, she went about the delicate task as quickly as she could. Five switches had to be flipped in a precise order first to arm the bomb. Then the timer had to be activated; she would set it for ten minutes, giving her time to place the bomb within the tunnel and contact the Klingon ship to have herself beamed back. Then the timer switch had to be pressed, to set the entire process in motion—and finally, the failsafe button must be pressed, so that any further attempts to disarm the bomb would set it off immediately.

As she knelt beside the bomb, setting its controls, she heard a slight sound behind her. Whirling quickly, she saw a guard standing in the doorway with some unfamiliar handweapon pointed directly at her. The young Romulan must have noticed this door ajar and come to investigate. Metika knew in that instant that she was a dead woman, and wished she'd never been so foolish as to allow Kolvor to talk her into this rash venture in the first place.

The Romulan was clearly not about to show any mercy for what was obviously an act of sabotage. The Terran female was only a few meters away, an easy target, as he lifted his gun and fired. But nothing happened. The streak of blue energy that should have streamed from the barrel of his weapon failed to materialize—and neither the Romulan nor Metika could quite believe it. The guard looked at his gun in amazement, then pointed it once again at the intruder and fired. The result was the same.

While this was going on, Metika recovered from her momentary paralysis. She was not sure how she could explain her sudden good fortune, but for now she would rather use it than question it. She reached for the phaser in her own holster, hoping to fire at the Romulan before he had another chance to kill her.

The guard, realizing his weapon was not going to work, tossed it aside and advanced toward Metika even as she aimed her own phaser. He was tall and lanky, with long arms, and he was able to knock the phaser from her hands before she could press the firing button. She tried to stand up just as he grabbed her shoulders and called out to his comrades for assistance.

Metika was struggling fiercely to break his grip, while he in turn was trying to pin one or both of her arms behind her. The sound of other approaching footsteps in the hallway outside told Metika that more Romulans were coming; if she couldn't get free of this one soon, she'd be hopelessly outnumbered. With a vicious jerk, she brought a knee up into the guard's groin with satisfactory strength. The young man howled with pain and doubled over, but still had the presence of mind to keep his grip on her tunic. The two combatants tumbled roughly to the floor, completely entangled in one another.

Then, just before the other Romulans arrived, Metika and the guard vanished from the ship, leaving no trace of their existence behind.

Down on the planet, the parties from the three ships were feeling subdued and not a little tired from Enowil's latest "demonstration," as he called it. Despite McCoy's hypothesis, there was indeed sex on this planet; each of them had had ample proof of that in the last couple of hours. Kirk could only shake his head in amazement; not only had Enowil provided facilities for every known variation and desire, there were also some things available that Kirk, for all his vast experience in the subject, could never have conceived of.

Beside him, Spock was looking a little ashen, and the captain was immediately concerned. "Are you all right?" he asked his first officer.

"I'll be fine, Captain," Spock replied. "It is interesting, though, how Enowil was able to trigger within me the frenzies of *pon far* without its being anywhere near the seven-year point in my cycle."

Kirk could not resist a small smile. "I don't notice you complaining, though."

"Complaint would be inappropriate, Captain. I merely note it as interesting."

Kirk glanced around at the rest of his party. Both Scotty and McCoy were grinning like the canaries that ate the cat. Sulu looked smug; Chekov was trying to be nonchalant, but only succeeded in looking embarrassed. Uhura was positively beaming as she radiated a sultry purr, and Metika ...

Metika was nowhere to be seen. Kirk quickly scanned the faces of his own group to make sure he hadn't missed her, then began craning his neck to see whether she might have gotten mixed up temporarily in one of the other groups. He realized with a start that he couldn't recall the last time he'd seen her.

Commander Probicol was speaking, and Kirk was momentarily distracted from his search. "As pleasant as these diversions are, they are diversions only. No wonder you cannot tolerate this place—it is completely predictable, at least to you. Everything happens according to your will, so there can be no surprises. There is no sense of the unexpected, no adventure."

Enowil looked hurt. "The day shall not be up so soon as I, to try the fair adventure of tomorrow," he said. "How can you possibly accuse me of such a thing? Why, adventures occur almost daily on this wonderful world. There is one to begin almost as we speak. Come, take my hand and let me lead you from the unreal to the real, from darkness to light, from death to immortality, and not into temptation."

Their host danced merrily away from them, and once more the three groups could do nothing but follow his lead lest they be left behind. Kirk twisted around as best he could, but still could not catch any glimpse of Metika. Eventually he gave up trying. She *had* to be here somewhere; there was nowhere else she could go but back up to the ship, and she would be safe enough there if she had.

Enowil led them out of the building once more, into an open field filled with tall, waving grain of a kind unfamiliar to Kirk. Probably quadrotriticale, he thought sarcastically, remembering how much trouble *that* had caused him in the past. There was a slight breeze in the air with the faintest tang of ozone. "Spock's gold star" was still well up in the sky.

The groups stood in the open field and waited. After almost five minutes of nothing happening, Commander Probical said irritably, "Where is the adventure you promised us?"

"Patience," Enowil said. "Waiting is."

"Waiting is what?"

"You wanted unpredictability, Commander. If I could predict exactly when it would begin, it would scarcely be an adventure, would it? You're not consistent if you . . . ah, here we go. I think it's about to start."

Over the horizon, a black speck appeared in the sky. It grew larger as it approached, until finally the people in the field could see that it was a large mauve dragon, flapping ungracefully about on an enormous pair of batwings. In its claws it carried a beautiful and seminude young lady with a crown upon her head. As it flew by, the dragon peered scornfully down at the group and breathed fire at them. The flames did not quite reach them, but smelled more of orange-blossoms than of brimstone.

The dragon passed overhead, with its captive yelling her plaintive pleas for help, and had started off in another direction when a second figure appeared on the horizon. This one approached the observers much more slowly, but after some time they could see that it was a young man on horseback. The fellow had noble features—obviously a hero—and was clad in full armor except that he lacked a helmet. Both sword and shield were strapped tightly to his horse's side; instead of a heraldic device, the shield was decorated with a large black and yellow bull's-eye, slightly off-center. The rider paid scant heed to the assembled watchers, keeping his eyes instead on the distant and diminishing figure of the dragon. Soon both the knight and the dragon were lost to view once more over the horizon.

"You call that an adventure?" Scotty asked. "That's one o' the oldest stories imaginable!"

"If you wanted *original* adventure, you should have come on Tuesday," Enowil sniffed. "Most adventures naturally replay the same motifs over and over. Tuesdays are when I experiment. Most of the experiments don't work out, of course—the heroine might be much likelier to marry the dragon, for instance—but I do keep trying. I admit this particular adventure has some stale ingredients to it, but perhaps it will still turn out well."

"Perhaps? Don't you know?"

"Of course not, my good sir. Did you think my adventures were *rigged?* That would be cheating. An adventure is only an adventure because you don't know how it will come out; otherwise it becomes merely an exercise in creative destiny. Come, the stage is set; shall we at least see what happens to our players?"

His question was rhetorical only; he gave the observers no time to reply. A box of force materialized around them, its walls shimmering and slightly tinged with blue, but mostly transparent. The energy box lifted off the ground and zoomed off after the principal characters in Enowil's adventure.

They caught up with them quickly enough, but it was clear that the Hero was going to have no easy time rescuing the Princess. The dragon was just now disappearing into a cave high up on the side of a mountain while, across the plain leading to that mountain, an army of sinister creatures waited to defend the dragon's lair against this sole interloper. The defenders came in a variety of types: some were fully armored knights like the Hero, others were samurai warriors; some were orcs and trolls, some were ghosts and wizards; many were misshapen creatures for which no name readily came to mind. All of them were determined, though, to keep the Hero from his appointed rounds.

"Now's when it starts getting exciting," Enowil told his audience.

If the Hero was daunted by the array of evil forces facing him, he did not show it. Taking his sword and his shield from their lashings on the side of his horse, he charged directly at the oncoming forces, determined that nothing should keep him from the side of his beloved. As he rode, he uttered a ferocious battlecry which must have struck fear into the heart of even his bravest foe.

The legion of his enemies parted momentarily to let him enter their midst, then closed around him once again. Certain now that they had their victim just where they wanted him, the ungodly hordes attacked the one rider, emitting cries of their own almost as ferocious as his. They advanced with swords, claws, fangs, and all manner of other deadly weapons both natural and artificial.

The Hero twirled his mighty blade once around his head, then began whacking great strokes at the enemy. For each cut and slash he made another foe fell, yet so great was their number that they continued despite their losses. The Hero's sword was dripping with blood—red, blue or black depending on the nature of the creature he killed. At one point his horse was felled from beneath him and he was tossed to the ground, but he managed to land on his feet, maintain his equilibrium and continue his fight. For a lone man on foot, though, the odds ranged against him were insuperable.

Then suddenly the air was rent by the blare of a trumpet and the thunder of hoofbeats, and over the horizon came a battalion of horsemen, all dressed in the uniforms of nineteenth-century American cavalry. A cry of dismay went up from the evil army surrounding the Hero as they whirled to face this unexpected threat. Their surprised reaction cost a few of them their lives as the Hero, encouraged by his newfound allies, swung his sword with renewed vigor and mowed down even more of his adversaries.

Within minutes, the battle had turned into a rout as the cavalry made short work of its opponents. The dragon's forces, cowardly as they were, did not want to stand and fight against an equal force; they turned and fled in disorderly array, leaving the field to the triumphant Hero and his cavalry allies.

The feeling of victory was short-lived, however, as the earth began to tremble to the sound of enormous footsteps. Out from behind the mountain where the dragon lived came a team of giants, ten of them, each one six stories tall and armed with a massive wooden club. Behind them, overhead, flew a squadron of creatures that looked like a cross between a pterodactyl and a roc. Their leathery, batlike wings stretched for a span of almost ten meters, and they had narrow, pointed heads and lidless eyes that focused relentlessly on their prey.

With ear-piercing screeches, the flying creatures began making low swoops at the cavalry. The horses, frightened by the attacks of these monsters, began rearing wildly, tossing their riders to the ground. The cavalry officers tried firing at the creatures with their old-style revolvers and rifles, but the bullets had little effect on such supernatural beings. And while they were attempting to deal with the menace from the air, the giants were advancing ever onward, covering the distance between themselves and the mortals with enormous ground-devouring strides.

Clearly the situation appeared hopeless, but still the Hero was not daunted. Laying his sword down upon the ground before him, he knelt and bowed his head, hands clasped together at his chest.

"What's he doing now?" one Klingon asked, breaking the silence that had covered the group so far.

"Praying, of course," Enowil replied. When the Klingon snorted his derision, the gnome continued, "Never underestimate the efficacy of prayer—you never know which god may be listening. In this case, since I am the god for this local section of reality, I have the responsibility to listen and answer him. The question is, should I interfere or let him take his chances on his own?"

"Oh, please help him," Lieutenant Uhura said. "He's so brave he deserves to win."

"But it's not fair," responded the Klingon who'd asked the original question. "If he's not capable of fighting the menace on his own, he doesn't deserve to win. Bravery is at best a fool's virtue."

"I don't recall saying an adventure had to be fair," Enowil replied with some surprise. "Am I some cosmic accountant who keeps a tally book of pluses and minuses to ensure that everything works out to some arbitrary zero point you call 'fair'? When you're a god, you're forced to look at the Big Picture. You don't have time to consider such trivialities as 'fair' and 'unfair,' 'right' or 'wrong.' Was it 'fair' that there should be ten giants instead of one? Who's to say?"

"But you'd be violating your own rules about the predictability of an adventure if you affect the outcome the way you want to," the Romulan commander argued.

"Self-consistency is a virtue chiefly among the unimaginative," Enowil said. "Every adventure is entitled to one miracle, and I've been far behind my quota of late, anyhow. Let's see, what would make a good deus ex machina?" Enowil took off his pointed cap for a moment and scratched his head. "Ah, ha! I know. I'll send him an avatar."

Down on the battlefield below, the flying monsters were killing many of the cavalrymen and the giants were almost upon the Hero. Suddenly there was a puff of green smoke and a figure appeared beside the kneeling knight. This newcomer's face looked very much like Enowil's, but the man was much taller and clad in long purple robes, upon which were embroidered golden runes and mystic symbols.

"Who's that?" asked Ensign Chekov.

"That is Roald the Invisible, sort of a watered down version of myself. Much less powerful, of course—it wouldn't do at all to make things too easy. But he is nonetheless an important sorceror."

"If he's invisible, how come I can see him?" McCoy asked.

"All questions must be submitted in writing at least one half hour before curtain time," Enowil replied testily.

On the plain below them, Roald the Invisible conferred briefly with the Hero and the cavalry leader, then set quickly to work to alleviate the dire situation. He waved his hands about his head, in much the same manner that Enowil sometimes used, meanwhile mumbling great spells and invoking miscellaneous spirits of air, earth and fire. Everyone, both on the ground and in Enowil's group of observers, waited to see what would happen next; this promised to be quite a show.

Nor were they disappointed. The flying monsters continued their aerial attacks, and the giants were almost within striking distance before anything happened. Suddenly, though the sky had been clear blue up until now, storm clouds rolled in—so rapidly that in less than a minute they covered the heavens with their massive grayness. The air flashed and crackled with thunder and lightning; the atmosphere was so charged that people's hair stood on end. Jagged thunderbolts, seeming alive, ripped downward toward the flying creatures; whenever one hit, the beast would explode in a cloud of static electricity, raining a shower of blue and red sparks down upon the plain below.

The giants, however, were not much affected by the celestial fireworks, and they brushed aside the lightning bolts as though they were so many pesky insects. The titans bellowed their war cries so loudly the whole earth shook, and swung their mighty clubs above their heads as they prepared to rain havoc down upon the hapless mortals below.

Roald the Invisible was busily making still more passes at the air with his hands, but they seemed hurried, as though even this master sorceror could not work fast enough to cope with the current crisis. Then, suddenly, with one climactic pass, the ground trembled and a rift opened between the mortals and the giants. Out of this chasm came a dozen huge beasts, looking vaguely like prehistoric monsters from a child's nightmare. Sensing the giants as their natural enemies, these mammoth creatures did not even bother with the puny humans standing on the plain; instead, with raucous cries, they converged on the club-wielding giants.

The battle raged fiercely for more than half an hour, as the titans and their reptiloid adversaries wrestled one another to the death. The Hero and his cavalry cohorts could only stand around gaping; without their mounts, they knew they could never run fast enough to elude pursuit should the giants win. The outcome of this fantastic battle was in doubt up till the last few tragic moments; sometimes a giant would fall victim to the slashing teeth of a monster, and sometimes the saurian would die from a skull wound administered by a vicious slash of a giant's club.

But in the end, Roald's wizardry proved the greater. There was one giant left to fight off two of the enormous beasts. As he swung wildly at one, the second leaped at his throat, sinking its fangs deep into the flesh and pulling the struggling giant to the ground with it. From that point on, it was no contest. The two huge beasts were more than a match for their foe, and soon the giant lay still. The victors began to fight between themselves over which would get to eat the kill, totally ignoring the Hero and the remnants of the cavalry watching the battle.

"I think," said Captain Kirk, "we've seen enough of this adventure."

"But it's a long way from over," Enowil protested. "The Hero hasn't even reached the cave yet, the one where the dragon took the Princess. You can never tell what sort of exciting things will be lurking about inside a cave."

Kirk did not particularly care, but he was learning not to voice such sentiments aloud for fear of wounding Enowil's feelings once again. "We're trying to think of a solution to your problem," he said, "but it's almost impossible with distractions like that going on around us."

Enowil sighed. "I suppose you're right. The adventures will go on without us, but sometimes they take strange directions if I'm not around to supervise. I do regret, though, not knowing how it all comes out."

13

At first, Metika felt disoriented as the Romulan ship
blinked out of existence around her. She and the
Romulan guard with whom she'd been struggling were
in a hazy limbo, and there was a dizzying feeling,
worse than freefall, gnawing at her head and
stomach. Her first thought was that the bomb she'd
planted must have gone off prematurely and blown
them away from the ship; but then she realized that
if the bomb had gone off she would currently be in
millions of tiny pieces, none of which would be capable of protracted thought processes.

Then, almost before she was completely aware of
her ghostly surroundings, they vanished as abruptly
as they had come, leaving her and her companion
back in the "real" world once more. They were not,
however, aboard the ship they had left a scant moment ago, but were sprawled instead on the smooth
floor in a dimly lit area. Metika propped herself up
on one elbow to have a better look around.

The Romulan who'd accompanied her was moaning
on the ground a meter away. He was still suffering
from the effects of the knee-blow to the groin she had
given him; the pain from that, and the dizziness of
the limbo they had passed briefly through, had finally
caused him to release his grip on her tunic, and his

writhing had separated their entangled bodies. He would be no threat to her in the immediate future.

But where were they? That was the problem of the moment. It took a few seconds for her eyes to become adjusted to the dimmer light of this place, but once they did and she could see around her, the surroundings were not at all familiar. The design did not appear similar to either the Romulan ship or the Klingon ship, both of which she'd been aboard only briefly. It was quite definitely not the *Enterprise;* no Federation vessel she'd ever heard of looked anything like this. By the process of elimination, that meant they were probably somewhere on Enowil's planet—but as for what *that* meant, no rational person could say for certain.

To one side, a wall towered kilometers over their heads. It was built of flat, unpainted wood and was braced by enormous slanted beams that were anchored into the smooth stone floor some distance away. The ceiling—if indeed this place had one—was lost to view in the distance above, but more immediately overhead, at a height of perhaps four or five meters, was a series of catwalks, crisscrossing in a veritable maze. There were stairs that occasionally ascended from the floor to the catwalks, and everywhere there were ropes—dangling from the catwalks, dangling from the walls, dangling from other places so high up that Metika could not see their origins.

It looked to her very much like the backstage area of some theater. A theater on this cosmic a scale would take some doing—but then, Enowil rarely seemed to think in anything but grandiose terms.

Getting to her feet now, Metika tilted her head back and tried once again to see whether there was a roof over her head. She did not appear to be outdoors—the light from overhead was not the bright blue of this world's daylight sky—but staring into the infinite only served to make her dizzy once again. She tried next looking on the other three sides away from the high, flat wall, but could see no other enclosures. This, apparently, was a backstage that went on forever.

Something hit her from behind, and she toppled unexpectedly forward. In her curiosity about her surroundings, she had forgotten entirely about the young Romulan guard who was trapped here with her. The man had recovered sufficiently from the pain and disorientation to renew his attack; perhaps he possessed less imagination and was not as concerned about where they were. He knew only that this woman was his enemy, and that he must stop her at all costs.

He was on top of her as they both hit the floor again, pummeling her with his fists and trying to land a decisive blow. She instinctively put her arms up to protect her face, and squirmed around on the floor trying to shake him loose from her. Finally, after nearly a minute of desperate wrestling, she managed to twist away and scramble to her feet. She could see, though, that the Romulan was determined; he was crouching again, prepared for another leap.

"Hey, wait," Metika said. "Truce. Let's talk this thing over."

The Romulan did not listen, and lunged at her instead. Metika sidestepped and just barely avoided him, but in the maneuver lost her balance and fell to the ground anyway. The man, realizing his misjudgment, tried to twist around and grab her; Metika had to roll to avoid his grasp.

Both young people were panting heavily as they stared across the empty space at one another for a moment, gathering their strength for another bout. "Please," Metika panted as she scrambled back to her feet. "We're both in the same predicament. We have to work together for the moment and forget ..."

"Forget? Can I forget that you're a treacherous, cowardly Terran who wanted to blow up my ship, with me in it?"

"For the moment that's all past. We don't know

where we are or what our situation is. We could be in terrible danger right now. We have to work together."

The Romulan's answer was a snarl as he got to his feet and charged at her again. Realizing that there was no alternative, that this young Romulan was in no mood to listen to reason, Metika sighed and stood her ground. She waited patiently as the young man came toward her, stepping deftly aside only when it was too late for him to check his charge. As she did so, she launched her fist squarely into his oncoming face. The impact jarred her arm clear up beyond the shoulder and spun her around—but its effect on the Romulan was worse. He dropped leadenly to the ground with a cut across his left cheek just below the eye.

"Ow!" Metika cried, shaking her hand in an attempt to relieve some of the pain. "I think I busted a couple of knuckles. I didn't know hitting someone like that could hurt so much."

The Romulan was conscious, but his eyes were not quite focusing. He groaned and tried to push himself up off the floor, but he was too stunned. He collapsed again on the ground and lay there, gathering his strength.

"Sorry I had to do that," Metika said. She cradled her sore right hand tenderly in her left. "My father was a space scout, and he showed me a few fighting tricks. This is the first time I ever actually used one—and I hope it's the last." She looked plaintively down at her throbbing hand. "Ow, that hurts."

"It . . . it's not too good from here, either," the Romulan panted weakly.

"It's your fault. You didn't want to listen. Care to listen now?"

The only response was silence, so she continued, "Well, I guess you can't do much else at the moment. My name is Metika Spyroukis, and you have every right to be mad at me. I could very easily have killed you with that bomb. I normally don't do things like that, honest. I don't know what came over me."

She paused and gave a sardonic little laugh. "Or maybe I do. There was that smooth-talking Klingon captain, and my father's recent death, and my concern for my friends who could be dying of argon poisoning right now—it's a number of things. I'm back to normal again—I think. An apology doesn't do any good, I know, but I wanted you to know I'm not trying to offer any excuses—just reasons."

The Romulan still did not say anything, though more definite signs of awareness were creeping into his eyes. He stared at her with a long look of loathing.

"Go ahead and hate me," Metika said. "I can hardly blame you, and I deserve it. But get it through that armor-plated head of yours that no matter how much you detest me, we have to work together for now. We've been transported somehow to . . . I don't know, to some strange place that may only exist in Enowil's imagination. Enowil *says* everything's harmless on this world, but his idea of harmless and mine are two entirely different things. And especially since we're away from the main group, he might not have this area as tightly under his control as the rest of them."

Even she had to shiver at the thought of what this world might become if Enowil ever let it get out of control.

"Come on, I know you Romulans have your stern code of honor, but can't you at least be civilized at the same time? I've told you my name; is yours supposed to be a secret?"

The Romulan was still looking at her bitterly, but her line of chatter seemed to be having its desired effect. The animal ferocity was disappearing from his features, letting something more of his true self shine through. In looking at him more closely, Metika noticed for the first time that he was actually about her own age—a young, if intense, man with light brown hair and intelligent eyes. His face, when not seething with rage and hatred, could not be called unpleasant.

"Marcus Claudius Breccio," he said crisply, almost spitting the words at her.

"Thank you. Now, Marcus Claudius Breccio, would you care to offer any guesses about where we are?"

The young man looked around him as though seeing his surroundings for the first time. Clearly he was awed by what he saw, and Metika had to remind herself consciously that he had not been part of the Romulan team on the planet; he was not used to the immense scale on which Enowil worked, nor to the skewed logic of the mad Organian. This entire situation did take some getting used to.

When Breccio did not answer after a moment, Metika offered her own hypothesis. "Enowil, the Organian who created this place, builds elaborate structures to impress the rest of us. According to what we know about Organians, they build their fantasy images out of pure thought energy—which means they must keep thinking about something or it will dissolve back into its original form. On a world as complex as this one I don't think even an Organian could think about all of it all the time. He has to have some props to help him—and I think we've somehow landed backstage, behind all the mystery. This is where he stores his magic until he's ready to use it— but some of it can be very dangerous if Enowil isn't around to control it. That's why we have to work together and help each other, at least until we can rejoin our own groups."

"And then what?"

Metika paused for a deep breath and a moment's thought. "All right, let's formalize our truce. As long as we're stranded here together, apart from our own people, we will cooperate to survive. As soon as we're reunited with the parties from our own ships, all bets are off and we have no further responsibilities to help one another. We can still be enemies when it's all over. I think that's fair. Is it a deal?"

The Romulan climbed slowly to his feet, still a bit wobbly, and studied her intensely. Finally he bent his right elbow so that his arm was across his chest with the flattened palm pointing downward—the Romulan gesture of oath-taking. "I pledge my honor," he said. "I warn you, though—the instant we're out of this, you'll be dealt with as the cowardly saboteur you are."

Metika shrugged. She had expected no more than that, and her conscience was telling her that she would deserve any punishment that came due. "Let's worry about getting out of here," she said.

As they both looked around, they could see only one barrier: the flat "wall" that towered above their heads. On the other three sides, the appearance of a backstage area continued on as far as they could see, disappearing into the dim lighting that came from *somewhere* in the darkness up above. "Which direction do you want to try?" Metika asked her reluctant ally.

Breccio studied the situation. "We can't climb the wall," he answered brusquely. "We'll either have to walk parallel to it or in the opposite direction from it. All three look equally bleak. Perhaps if we climbed up onto one of those catwalks we could see a little further and get some clue which way to proceed."

Maybe there's hope for him yet, Metika thought. So far, she had not been impressed with her companion's intelligence, but his plan did make sense. At the very least it would get them moving; nothing would be accomplished by just standing here and talking. She nodded agreement and they started off.

The two strode over to a ladder leading up to the catwalks. Breccio was still a little shaky from the punch; Metika offered her hand to steady him, but he spurned her offer and walked proudly on his own. They climbed upward in silence and stood for a moment surveying the scene around them. Disappointingly it was identical to the view they'd seen from the ground—this same odd emptiness stretching on forever in three directions, the flat wall towering up higher than they could see in the fourth.

Metika turned to speak to Breccio when suddenly the air was split by a piercing shriek. It was hard to tell direction at first, and she looked wildly around through the gloom, attempting to see what could possibly have made that sound. Then the keening came again, and they both realized that it was coming from above them. Metika and Breccio looked up and, almost as one, gasped in surprise and fear at what they saw.

Diving out of the sky straight at them was a creature born of nightmares. Its batlike wings spread to a span greater than a three-story building; lidless eyes stared at them, and the long pointed beak seemed like a spear descending. The beast let out yet another raucous cry and opened its beak, exposing to their view double rows of small, razorsharp teeth. Its leathery skin looked tough as it extended its claws to grab at them and rend them apart.

Metika backed instinctively away, but Breccio stood stock still. At first the girl thought her companion had been petrified by fear, but then realized that he was looking around for something to use as a weapon. There was nothing handy, so he turned back to her. "Down!" he shouted.

At the same time, to make sure she obeyed him, he gave her a push that sent her tumbling under the rickety railing toward the floor. An instant later he had dived off as well, following her down even as the creature's talons were raking the air where they had just been standing.

"But love is not fashionable any more," Enowil was saying. "The poets have killed it. They wrote so much about it that nobody believed them."

"Then call it affection, if you prefer," Lieutenant Uhura said, undaunted. "But it's something I think you're lacking here. For all the people that you showed us crowding around, for all the arguing, for all the sex, I still haven't seen one sign of basic love and affection. Perhaps someone of your own kind . . ."

"I came here to get away from people of my own kind."

"You're evading the question," Dr. McCoy said. "Uhura's right—we all need something to soothe our psyches every so often, someone or something to whom we matter. If not another person, then at least a favorite pet."

"Now that you mention it," Enowil said, reaching into a hitherto-unsuspected pocket, "I have something here that might just do the trick. You may have seen something like this before."

The small furry object he held in his hand looked suspiciously familiar to the people from the *Enterprise*. "Is your planet, then, infested with tribbles, too?" Spock asked.

"Hardly infested," Enowil answered. "When I make tribbles, I make them properly. These little darlings do not eat, do not reproduce, and do not grow. They merely purr and give you all the love and affection you could possibly demand. What more could any sentient being ask?"

Commander Probicol's communicator buzzed at that moment, and the Romulan leader excused himself and stood a few paces away to receive a message from his ship. There had been an intruder aboard, and Lieutenant Breccio had intercepted the person before any harm could be done. Both Breccio and the intruder had disappeared, though, without a trace; the officer in charge back on the ship assumed that the two had been beamed back aboard whichever ship the invader had come from—but there was no evidence left to indicate which ship that might be.

Probicol scowled. He remembered only too well Captain Kolvor's approach, trying to enlist his aid in sabotage against the *Enterprise*. The stench of that offer still insulted his nostrils; few Romulans would

ever stoop to such underhanded tactics. If there was
attempted sabotage against him now, it was obviously
a Klingon attempt at revenge for his refusal.

But would Kolvor do such an act on his own?
Probicol had had a few dealings with Klingons before,
and had yet to find a one he thought had any honor
or courage. Kolvor was too much of a coward to
attack the Romulan vessel directly; he would find
some way to induce others to perform his dirty work
for him.

Probicol had thought the Federation captain, Kirk,
was, if nothing else, a man of honor. Perhaps that
was a misjudgment. With the stakes as high as they
were now, anyone with less than Romulan integrity
might be seduced into trying to better his own odds.
Or perhaps this Kirk had thought up the scheme independently.

At the moment, though, the question of who was
behind the attack was of secondary importance. War
had been declared, a silent war of stealth and sabotage. One of Probicol's crewmembers had been taken,
and must be presumed dead. If Probicol came out
and accused one or both of the other parties, they
would roundly deny it—and he had no evidence yet
to prove otherwise, merely the word of his crewmembers back aboard the *Talon*.

But there had to be some other way of striking
back. Whoever had been responsible, he would now
know that his attack had failed, and would be expecting retaliation of some sort. Probicol decided to try
the game of patience; let his opponent—or opponents—wait and worry for a while. Expectation, after
all, was the choicest part of fear.

After sending Metika off on her mission of destruction, Captain Kolvor returned to the party down
on the planet, insinuating himself back into the group
as though he'd never been away. He wanted to be
here when the Romulan ship was destroyed, so that
he could look as innocent and surprised as everyone

else. He watched the adventure of the Hero on the plain with the rest of them, awaiting any moment the news of the *Talon*'s destruction.

As the adventure wore on, however, and no news came, he realized that something must have gone wrong. The Federation woman must have been spotted and either killed or captured by the Romulans; even now she could be undergoing the grueling interrogation he knew the Romulans were capable of, and he had little doubt she would immediately try to implicate him in the plot.

Kolvor smiled inwardly as he congratulated himself on his foresight. Convincing the Terran woman to plant the bomb for him was a stroke of genius, even if he did have to admit it himself. When Probicol came out and accused him, Kolvor would have his defense all ready. Of course the Terran woman would try to fasten the blame on him, Kolvor would say. One would hardly expect her to implicate her own captain, would one? The Federation and the Klingons were enemies, everyone knew that. How likely was it that they would be working together? But, on the other hand, how likely was it that she would try to drag one of her enemies down with her? Any rational being would have to conclude that she was naming Kolvor purely out of spite, in a feeble attempt to make herself look a little better.

When the call came down to Probicol from the *Talon*, Kolvor was prepared for the worst. He studiously avoided watching the Romulan commander, paying close attention to every syllable Enowil spoke while bracing himself for the inevitable denunciation. But none came. Probicol finished his conversation with his ship and returned to the group as though nothing whatsoever had gone wrong.

Kolvor was puzzled. Could the woman have been killed during her attempt to plant the bomb? In that event, the Federation would be the only ones implicated in the plot—even better for him. The only thing that might point a finger of suspicion in the

Klingon direction would be the distinctive design of the bomb itself. But Kolvor was prepared to argue that the Federation knew perfectly well what Klingon bombs looked like, and had deliberately constructed this one in such a manner to throw everyone off the track. Kolvor was covered from all directions, and felt very satisfied with himself.

The satisfaction did not last long. Probicol made no attempt to denounce the Federation *or* the Klingons. Yet he surely must know something had happened; the fact that the *Talon* was still in existence meant that the plan had been foiled, that the woman had been detained in her efforts. Probicol would certainly be within his right to complain to Enowil; why didn't he?

This was serious, and Kolvor devoted a good deal of thought to it over the next few hours.

14

Metika and Breccio fell toward the ground as the nightmarish pterodactyl screamed and dove at them. Unprepared for the shove Breccio had given her, Metika fell clumsily; she was frightened out of her wits both by the prospect of the fall and by the peril descending from above. The instinctive fear of falling robbed her momentarily of her reason as she braced herself for the inevitable collision with the hard ground; but even so, a small part of her mind, way in the back, was telling her that she was falling at a slightly slower speed than she expected.

She nonetheless hit the floor with a heavy thump and rolled slightly to one side. That small additional motion saved her from possible serious injury as Breccio came down within centimeters of her. They had no time to think or react beyond that, however; the powerful stench of the large flying monster was already overpowering them as its sharp beak snapped at the air.

But the huge creature was not constructed to maneuver in such crowded conditions as this "backstage" area. When the two people jumped from their perch, the pterodactyl experienced a moment of hesitation, knowing it would be difficult for a being of its size to pry such small creatures out from under the maze of catwalks. It then tried to pull out of its dive, but it had already committed itself and the brief moment of hesitation had sealed its doom. With wings outstretched, it emitted a blood-curdling shriek and crashed headlong into the structure of the catwalks.

There was a massive ripping sound as the wooden structures twisted and split apart under the force of the collision. Flurries of torn ropes and a shower of broken boards rained down on the ground; a shattered segment of bannister lodged itself in the creature's chest, killing it instantly. The dead monster was wedged into place, suspended in the air as though still trying, after death, to menace the two people on the ground.

Metika did not realize she'd closed her eyes until she had to open them. When she did so, she saw that Breccio had rolled on top of her after landing. Whether it had been a conscious action to save her from falling debris or just an automatic response she could not say, but suddenly she found herself staring directly up into the face of the Romulan.

Their eyes met for a long second, then quickly looked away again—as though both of them were responding to a set of unspoken cues. The Romulan realized quite suddenly that he was lying in much too intimate a manner atop the body of a woman from the hated Federation. He pushed himself away and got quickly to his feet as though the contact had been odious—though, if he had bothered to be honest with himself, he would not have minded it nearly as much as he pretended.

"Thank you," Metika said, the softness of her voice surprising even her.

"We agreed to help one another, didn't we?" Breccio replied brusquely. He was angry, but more at himself than at anything else—and it made him even angrier not knowing why he should be. "I was merely living up to my agreement."

"Yes. Of course. I'm sorry if I gave the impression there were any other motives involved."

"One does not need expressions of gratitude for fulfilling one's responsibilities," the Romulan continued stiffly.

"I already apologized. Isn't that enough?" Metika, too, got to her feet and began brushing the dust off her clothes.

"We must remember that we are enemies, forced to cooperate only by the most unusual of circumstances. When this is over, we will be enemies again. Nothing can change that."

"You've made your point abundantly clear," Metika said, irked by the Romulan's single-mindedness. "Now if I may make a suggestion, it might be wise to get out from under that thing; I don't want to be buried if it collapses onto the ground."

Breccio looked upward and realized what she was talking about. The pterodactyl was suspended above them, entangled in the remains of the catwalk network—but it was swaying precariously, as though any second might see it tumbling down on top of them. Taking the girl's advice, he walked briskly out from underneath the carcass, pausing only long enough to pick up a long piece of board that had broken off one of the catwalks. The board had a sharpened edge, and would suffice—barely—as a makeshift sword. "We may need some kind of weapon," he explained, and Metika nodded her consent.

Now that the momentary excitement of the dive bomb attack had ended, they were faced with the same problem they'd had before: which way to go to get out of here (wherever "here" was) and rejoin their comrades. Their brief survey from the catwalk had only convinced them that the job of leaving would be harder than they had originally supposed; and now there was the added difficulty that they must keep a sharp lookout against possible future attacks— either from more pterodactyls or from other, perhaps even more fearsome, creatures.

Breccio looked around them and came to a decision. "I think we might have the best luck walking parallel to this wall one way or the other. It has to end someplace, and then we can walk around it; if we tried walking away from the wall instead, we might go on forever before reaching anything."

The plan sounded logical to Metika, who pointed to the left. "Let's go that way, then, as long as we're choosing directions at random."

They began walking to the indicated direction. Their pace was slow; both were bruised from their fall off the catwalk, though astonishingly no bones had been broken and no muscles or joints had been twisted. Metika once again recalled the falling sensation and its apparent slowness, which had to be responsible for their good condition. Could that, too, be Enowil's doing? Was he still watching over them secretly, even here in this apparently deserted portion of the world? She could not say for certain, and she did not want to put that hypothesis to the test.

The two walked side by side, but by unspoken agreement kept a distance of almost a meter between themselves. They were not friends, the distance indicated, nor could they ever be; they came from enemy worlds, and must remain discreetly apart.

They had gone barely a hundred meters when Breccio held up a hand. "I thought I saw something move down there," he whispered, pointing straight ahead. "We'd better be careful."

To emphasize his words, he tightened his grip on the wooden "sword" he carried, holding it point outward, ready to thrust at an enemy if necessary. He moved away from the wall, toward the series of braces that supported it, so that he could remain at least partially hidden; Metika followed his example while still maintaining the social distance between them.

They stood there for a minute, not moving, hardly even daring to breathe, as they scanned the territory ahead. Then Metika, too, spotted a motion. She immediately pointed, and Breccio nodded agreement. They both knew there was something down there, and it was coming their way fairly quickly.

In another couple of minutes it had approached close enough for the pair in hiding to make out what it was. Metika had to stifle a gasp, and even Breccio looked slightly shaken. It put the girl in mind of the ogres in the fairy tales she'd read as a child. The being towered well over two meters tall and could not have weighed less than a hundred and fifty kilos. His beefy body was clad in some moth-eaten animal skins, and was almost as hairy as they were. Scraggly black hair hung over his close-set eyes, while two enormous tusks reached upward from his underslung jaw almost to the edge of his snoutlike nose. He carried a massive iron sword at the ready as though he, too, were expecting trouble.

Breccio was about to turn to Metika and suggest that they hide and hope the ogre would not see them when the matter was suddenly made academic. The ogre's piggy eyes, which had been darting back and forth across its path, lighted on the pair standing by the support. With a bellow of rage, he swung his sword in a full circle twice over his head and charged directly at the two smaller beings.

Metika and Breccio immediately separated, hoping to delay the other's attack by offering two different targets. The ogre, noticing that Breccio was the only one of the pair who appeared to be armed, turned and went after him; the other one, he reasoned, would be less of a threat and could be dealt with later.

Breccio backed away, trying to avoid a direct confrontation. He knew his broken board was no match for the ogre's iron blade; it couldn't even be used for parrying, for one whack from the real sword would shatter Breccio's weapon to pieces. He would have to stay out of the other's reach and pray for an opening that would allow him to use his flimsy weapon to advantage.

It was not an easy task. For all the ogre's immense size and bulk, he moved with amazing quickness and agility, and had a reach that covered large distances.

The smile on his bestial face was a grisly snarl of triumph as he watched his opponent dance away in fear.

Then tragedy struck. Breccio's foot caught on a slight irregularity in the floor just as he was back-pedaling away from the ogre's mighty swordstrokes. The Romulan fell backward onto the ground, and the ogre roared with delight. This would be the perfect chance to finish off his puny antagonist. Advancing savagely, he raised his sword with both hands above his head to administer the coup de grace.

Metika saw that she was facing a do-or-die situation. Unarmed as she was, there was nothing she could do to destroy the ogre; yet if she did nothing, Breccio would be dead and she would quickly follow him. Gathering her courage, she charged directly at the ogre's legs from behind, diving directly between them just as the creature was advancing on Breccio's helpless form.

She caught the ogre in midstride, just as one leg went forward while the other went back. She felt for an instant as though the scissors action might break her in two, but the ogre, unprepared for this attack from a new direction, stumbled over her and fell heavily to the ground. Breccio, recovering from his own fall just in time, rolled out of the way and scrambled to his feet as his foe hit the floor.

The Romulan did not give his opponent any opportunity to recover. The instant the monster was down, Breccio rushed over and thrust his jagged board as hard as he could into the ogre's neck. The board broke the first time without doing much damage, but the resultant fragment was even sharper. A second thrust was all it took. Blood spurted out of the wound, covering both Breccio and Metika liberally with the warm, sticky substance. The ogre twitched several times, then lay still.

Metika extricated herself carefully from between the ogre's legs and stood up, only to find Breccio staring at her. The Romulan looked quickly away again and opened his mouth to say something, but closed it with a snap.

"You're welcome," Metika said acidly.

"What?"

"Oh, I'm sorry. I thought you said 'Thank you.' "

"No, I didn't." Breccio still was not looking at her.

"Of course not. After all, one should not be thanked for doing one's duty. How foolish of me to forget."

Although he kept his face perfectly stern, Breccio could not prevent a blush from creeping over him; in the case of a Romulan, it amounted to a slight excess of green around the tips of his pointed ears.

To shift the conversation away from this sensitive subject, Breccio walked over and took the iron sword and he needed both hands to lift it, but it nevertheless from the dead ogre's hand. It was a heavy weapon, gave him a feeling of confidence he had not had since arriving in this strange place. "At least we have a real weapon now, in case anything else goes wrong," he said.

There was a popping noise over their heads, and they looked up, startled. They were afraid another of the giant pterodactyls might be diving at them, but instead it was only Enowil standing in midair some five meters above their heads. The funny-looking gnome glanced first at the dead ogre on the ground by their feet, then over into the distance at the carcass of the pterodactyl that was still suspended in air where it had rammed into the catwalks.

At length, the gnome shook his head and clucked regretfully. "I can't take you two anywhere, can I?" he said.

"Then you *are* responsible for bringing us here," Metika accused. "I knew this was your type of funhouse."

"Oh?" Enowil's eyebrows arched magnificently. "Are you having fun?"

"You know perfectly well what I meant," Metika

said, in no mood to parry words with him. "I demand that you take us back to our own people immediately."

"You'll have to speak up a bit," Enowil said. "I'm a trifle deaf in my right ear." But before Metika could say anything more, the mad Organian had vanished again with another loud *pop*, leaving them no better off than they'd been before.

"Arguing with him is like sifting air through a strainer," the girl grumbled, frustrated. "You end up feeling that nothing's been accomplished."

When Breccio did not reply immediately, Metika glanced over at him and found him staring upward into the gloom. She craned her head back so that she, too, could look at whatever he was seeing, and the sight made her gasp.

There, silhouetted against the hazy sky, was an enormous dragon flying past, clutching a weakly struggling princess in one massive, scaly claw.

The feast that was laid out before the assembled groups from the three ships was far beyond what might be fit for a king. No king in the history of any single planet could have afforded all the exotic dishes that were on the table, waiting to be sampled. There was nardhorn stuffed with tiny Melastin crayfish and covered with a thick wine-and-manzatine sauce; tiny dro-fowl, none bigger than a human thumb, roasted to a succulent brown; crisp Patastorian beef pasties; fine Romboid protein cakes with addleberry dressing; live crustamers duly exuding their pink, eggy secretion that was considered such a delicacy on the planet Ruffam; and hundreds upon hundreds of other specialties from all the major worlds throughout the known Galaxy.

The feast was spread upon long rectangular wooden tables in an immense hall more than a hundred meters long. Enowil had brought the group here in response to a suggestion that perhaps what was lacking in his life was the pleasure of gourmet dining.

Enowil was in the process of making the point that, while his energy body did not need the same kind of sustenance that physical bodies required, he could nonetheless supply himself with any delicacy so far found within the universe. After admitting that he had detained his guests too long without food, he invited them to partake of this feast at their own leisure. He disappeared briefly, but returned a moment later as chipper as ever.

Kirk wandered up and down the tables, sampling little bits from various dishes as though at an immense smorgasbord. The quality of the food was indeed the highest he'd ever tasted, but his mind was far from his palate. There were other curious events occurring than the ones that Enowil provided.

Both Probicol and Kolvor were behaving very strangely. During the past couple of hours, Kirk had noticed them watching him with unreadable expressions on their faces, although they looked away quickly enough when they realized he had noticed. They were also staring even more often at one another with expressions of calculating cunning. It was as though there were some sort of game going on, one to which Kirk had not received an invitation although the others assumed he knew the rules. He was curious to learn what it was, but for obvious reasons could not ask either party involved. In the end, he decided to flash knowing smiles to each, hoping they would think he knew more than he did.

He was also very puzzled by the disappearance of Metika Spyroukis. She was definitely no longer with the three parties that were following Enowil through this Wonderland. He had placed a quick call back up to the *Enterprise*, only to learn that she had not been beamed back aboard. Asking Enowil had been useless; the Organian had merely smiled and said, "While I am all-powerful and all-knowing, Captain, that doesn't mean I'm all-telling as well." The fact that Enowil was not worried could be interpreted as a good sign—but then, what did Enowil have to worry about? Metika's welfare was Kirk's responsibility, not his.

Kirk checked with his other officers, but none of them could precisely remember the last time they had seen Metika. The captain was pretty sure he and the girl had argued before Spock's game with the computer, but that had been several hours ago—and in the meantime, the Romulan and Klingon leaders had begun their unspoken game. Could Metika's disappearance have something to do with that? But what connection could there possibly be?

Kirk absently took a taste of a variety of food he'd never seen before. If things continued as they were for much longer, he would have to take some action to break through the silent game the Klingons and the Romulans were playing. He wasn't sure yet what form that action would take, but he did know that whatever it was, Kolvor and Probicol would remember it for a long time to come.

Captain Kolvor's confidence in the brilliance of his strategy had, by now, long since evaporated. There was no question but that the Romulans knew of the attempt against their ship. An attack by Probicol against the Klingons and/or the Federation should have followed. But to have the foray totally ignored was unsettling, to say the least.

To a Klingon like himself, waiting around for something to happen was an excruciating torture. Kolvor preferred to be taking direct action against his opponents, whatever the outcome might be. He dared not act against the Romulans again; the first attack would have put them on alert, and there was little chance of taking them by surprise a second time. The Enterprise, though, would make a slightly easier target. Being a bigger ship, there would be more places inside it for hiding—and, having no inkling of what had gone on, they were not as likely to be alert against the possibility of intruders.

He would not try, though, to find some willing

Romulan this time to do the job for him. Despite the advantages such a plan had, it held one enormous drawback: namely, that it depended entirely on the abilities of a member of one of the lesser races. It was obviously the Terran girl's incompetence that led to the failure of the first plan; Kolvor refused to make the same mistake twice. He reminded himself of the old Klingon motto: "Never trust an inferior to get the job done properly."

Next time, as soon as the opportunity presented itself, he would personally supervise the job. He called up to his ship and ordered his engineer to prepare another bomb.

15

The day turned out to be a long and wearing one for Metika and Breccio as they made their plodding way through the seemingly endless "backstage" area of Enowil's world. Metika had had nothing to eat or drink since leaving the *Enterprise* with the rest of the group, and her body was complaining loudly about her mistreatment of it. There were no toilet facilities back here, either; when privacy was needed, she would explain the situation to Breccio and walk a sufficient distance from the wall until she was behind one of the braces. Breccio, for all his crude Romulan ways, behaved in a gentlemanly manner and waited patiently for her to return before continuing. She returned the favor for him when necessary.

No matter how far they traveled, they could find little relief from the drabness of their surroundings. Catwalks and braces, ropes and sandbags seemed to be the universal decor. At one point they found a pit in the floor, filled with enormous gears and cog wheels —some more than five meters in diameter—all spinning and ticking away as though the entire world were running on clockwork. Metika refused to believe that; Enowil had probably put these in here merely for effect. The two travelers made their way around the pit and continued on after the detour as though nothing had interfered with the journey.

But if the landscape was monotonous, their journey itself was not. The pterodactyl and the ogre were only the first of the bizarre and dangerous beings they met along their odyssey. There was a fiery demon whose very touch would probably have proved fatal; a pair of animated skeletons with no organs to damage, who kept on fighting until their bones were broken apart and scattered over the ground; an orc in thick bronze armor; spectral creatures who were totally intangible, yet who could smother a living being by enveloping it within their shadowy forms; strange beasts with multitudinous limbs and indefatiguable appetites for human and/or Romulan flesh; and others, too, who seemed to run together after a while in Metika's memory.

Somehow, no matter how formidable their opponents seemed, the two travelers always managed to win their contests. The margin of victory was sometimes far too narrow for comfort, but they emerged unscathed from each battle. Secretly Metika formulated the theory that Enowil was watching them all along, deriving some vicarious thrills from observing their exploits but making sure things never got too far out of hand. She did not voice these thoughts aloud, however; for one thing, Enowil would hear them if she did and it might affect his behavior— and for another, she didn't want to let the pressure off Breccio. Her own continued welfare depended too much on him.

The young man was still a minor mystery to her, despite all the trials they were enduring together. Having been brought up with the rigid Romulan sense of ideals and duty, he abided faithfully by their promise of mutual assistance, and Metika knew he would continue to do so until they were out of danger. But beyond that, there was no saying. The Romulans were, after all, a distant offshoot of the Vulcan race, and reading their emotions was sometimes difficult. Breccio was clearly uneasy working so closely with an enemy of his people; if he felt cooperation was no longer necessary, might he not consider their pact terminated? That would return Metika once more to her status of saboteur—and she was only too aware that, in battle situations, the Romulans took no prisoners. She, as an enemy, would be killed outright.

She did nothing, then, to give Breccio any hint that their lives might not be in constant danger. The two young people talked but little as they wandered along through this shadowy world behind the "reality" Enowil had created for the others. Yet sometimes Metika could feel Breccio's eyes on her when he thought she wasn't looking—and there were also times when she found her own gaze wandering idly in his direction. *Well, why shouldn't I look at him?* she thought. *He's not that unpleasant to look at.*

For a Romulan, she added hastily.

She had no idea of how long they had been lost here behind the scenes; her watch had stopped after being jarred in the fall from the catwalk. All she knew was that it had been far too many hours since she'd had either food or rest, and she desperately needed both.

Then, quite suddenly, they came upon the door.

Although Enowil had allowed his other guests to take a break during their excursion, Kirk was feeling almost as weary and impatient as Metika was. No matter what anyone suggested for this world. Enowil already had it. True, the ways he had of demonstrating things were cockeyed and off-kilter, but they did work. Kirk and his crew were running out of things to think of—and so were the Romulans and the Klingons.

Kirk specifically consulted with Dr. McCoy. As a trained psychologist, the doctor would be the person who should have the most insight into Enowil's character; it was he who stood the best chance of figuring out why the Organian was unhappy and what it would take to cure the condition.

"I don't know, Jim," McCoy said, shaking his head. "There's something about him that I can't quite grasp. There've been isolated moments here and there when I saw a glimmering of something useful, but nothing I've been able to put into words yet. There is something he needs, I'm sure of that, but I'll need a little more time and thought before I can tell you exactly what it is."

"Time is what we don't have, Bones. The Klingons or the Romulans could come up with it at any second, and then we'll have lost. And then, there are the colonists on Epsilon Delta 4. We don't want to wait much longer or it'll be too late for them."

"I'll do what I can, Jim. That's all I can promise."

Kirk wandered off again, still deep in thought. The mention of Epsilon Delta 4 had brought the mystery of Metika Spyroukis to his attention once more. The explorer's daughter was still very much among the missing. She was not aboard the *Enterprise*, and the ship's sensors were able to account for every humanoid life form in this bubble of unreality except for her. It was as though she had ceased to exist anywhere—although Kirk knew that Enowil was perfectly capable of tricking the sensors so that they would not register her presence. Kirk was getting very tired of the Organian's circuitous tactics. Enowil must know very well where Metika was; why wasn't he telling anyone?

They were back on the planet now, seated in the stands of a large arena and looking down upon a scene of gladiatorial combat. One of the Romulans had suggested that Enowil might be lacking the thrill of spectator sports, and the Organian was demonstrating what he could purportedly do in that area of interest. The sight down on the field was worse than a four-ring circus. Several teams of men were wrestling barehanded. Other men were fighting in an apparent free-for-all with swords, morningstars, maces, battle-axes, pikes, nets and daggers. Another set was trying to subdue various wild animals. A group of athletes was running relay races back and forth across the field, using the other contenders as obstacles to be avoided. A final group was playing on the grass, a very involved game using three large balls, a racket, hoops, whistles and very special stomach pads. Kirk could not make the slightest bit of sense out of it, nor was he trying to. Once one became accustomed to Enowil's flare for the outré, his creations were really rather boring.

"And now, ladies and gentlemen, for the prime attraction," Enowil announced, with rather more pomp than the situation seemed to require. "I direct your attention to the central door."

Kirk looked over to the indicated spot, wondering what wonders Enowil would think of next. The far side of the arena was a large blank wall, rising up higher than Kirk could see. In the center of it, a large gilded door swung slowly open and two figures emerged. One looked like a Romulan and the other was ... Metika.

It took but an instant for the impression to register on his mind, and then Kirk was all action. Leaping from his seat, he bounded down the aisle into the arena, paying little attention to the competitions and combats. He ran straight to the girl from his ship and cried, "Metika! Are you all right?"

The girl and her Romulan companion looked dazed, as though they could not quite believe where they were. They stood frozen for an instant, muscles tensed as they observed the chaos occurring on the field around them. Then Metika saw Kirk running toward her and relaxed visibly. "At last," she said. "I was beginning to think we'd never find our way back."

"What happened? Where have you been? How did you get separated from us? Why is the Romulan with you? How did your clothes get so badly torn?" Now that he knew she was safe, Kirk's relief was being expressed in the barrage of questions that had been haunting him ever since the girl's disappearance.

Commander Probicol, in charge of the Romulan party, had also walked across the field when he saw his crewmember appear. He had moved more slowly than Kirk, with more dignity, and yet had somehow managed to cover the same distance in almost the same amount of time. "Perhaps Lieutenant Breccio will be able to answer those questions, Captain Kirk," he said.

Both ship's captains looked at the tall young Romulan questioningly. Metika, too, looked at him, an expression of anxiety on her lovely face. The truce between them was over now, and Breccio had sworn to treat her as a saboteur. She deserved no better, she knew. Hers had been a rash and foolish action. But still, she dreaded what he would say.

Breccio was looking most flustered for a Romulan. He opened his mouth twice to speak, closing it each time without a word. He pointedly did not look at Metika. Finally he managed to stammer out an answer. "I . . . I was aboard ship, checking out the engine room when suddenly I was transported to a place I did not recognize here on this planet. This Federation woman was there with me; I don't know where she came from." He went on from there to describe some of the adventures they had undergone backstage.

Metika listened to his recounting in shocked silence. Breccio was lying—for her. Despite what he had told her earlier, he was deliberately covering up her attempted sabotage so that his commander would not create an incident.

That was an awful risk, Metika was sure. With the Romulan attitude about duty so strongly ingrained, such lies would have to be considered a terrible offense. And yet he was lying to protect her. Why? Each had saved the other's life a number of times during their travels; any debt he owed her for saving him would have been cancelled out by his rescuing her. So why was he lying?

Commander Probicol listened to Breccio's story with his eyes narrowed. From his impatient stance, Metika was sure he did not believe everything Breccio was telling him. Nevertheless, the Romulan leader waited until his lieutenant was completely finished before he spoke. "That's all you wish to say?"

Breccio hesitated. "Well, there are more details if you'd like, sir, but I've covered the general outline."

"And you insist you never saw this woman before materializing on this world?"

"Yes sir, I do." Breccio's voice was a trifle shaky, and Metika had no confidence in its ability to fool anyone.

"Strange." Probicol stroked two fingers casually across his forehead in a gesture of assumed puzzlement. "Some of your fellow crewmembers distinctly heard you call out for help. Why was that?"

Breccio gulped. "I . . . I thought I saw something wrong on one of the dials, sir. I wanted someone else to come in and check my reading."

"I see. We found your weapon on the floor against one wall. How did that happen?"

"I dropped my stylus, sir. The weapon must have slipped from its holster as I bent over to retrieve it."

"You must have been very clumsy, Lieutenant."

"I'm afraid so, sir." Breccio was rigidly at attention, his eyes focused on infinity.

"We also found a Federation-style phaser on the floor. Did you drop that as well?"

Breccio did not answer, but sweat was starting to bead on his forehead.

"I notice that this woman's holster is empty. Could it be that the phaser came from there?"

Kirk had stood by silently so far during this inquisition, but now that the subject had turned so abruptly in the direction of one of his people, he felt obliged to speak up. "I warn you, Commander, not to make unsubstantiated charges against my crew or there'll be serious repercussions."

"Captain." Metika laid a hand softly on Kirk's arm. "Don't. I . . . He's right, I was there." She turned to Probicol. "Lieutenant Breccio is merely trying to protect me. I was in your engine room, and he caught me there."

Probicol spun to face her. There was a tight, smug smile on his face and a flash of fire in his eyes. "And what, pray tell, were you doing in our engine room?"

"You don't have to answer that, Metika," Kirk advised her. "At this time, in this place, he has no right to . . ."

Metika shook her head. "It's something I have to say. I feel so guilty about it now, so ashamed, that I have to get it out into the open." She squared her shoulders and looked the Romulan commander straight in the face. "I was trying to sabotage your ship by setting off a bomb in the engine room."

The Romulan commander merely nodded; that was the answer he'd been expecting. But Kirk looked stunned. "You what? Who gave you the authority? No one aboard the *Enterprise* would have beamed you onto the Romulan ship without orders from me."

"Are you trying to protest your innocence, Captain?" Probicol asked icily.

"He *is* innocent, Commander," Metika said. "I've told you the truth so far and I'm going to continue. It was Captain Kolvor who talked me into it, and I went along with him because . . . well, because I was in a hurry and I didn't stop to think rationally. That's not a good excuse and I'm not trying to use it as one. Kolvor took me up to his ship, gave me the bomb, showed me how to set it and beamed me onto the *Talon*. Lieutenant Breccio caught me and tried to stop me, and then we were suddenly transported here. The rest of his story is true."

Probicol gave a derisive snort. "Well, there's one way we can check your story—we'll see what the Klingon has to say." He turned to look for Kolvor.

But there was no sign of the Klingon captain.

16

When the Terran woman appeared in the arena, Kolvor knew that the time for immediate action had come. The Romulan commander and the Federation captain would be trading charges for a few minutes, but the girl would not fail to mention Kolvor's involvement in the affair and they would turn eventually to him for confirmation. When his plan was first put into operation he had been confident of talking his way out of any difficulties, but doubts had arisen in the intervening hours. Nothing was going the way he had planned it so far, and now, with panic setting in, he felt the need to take more drastic steps.

Fortunately, everyone's attention was focused on the two newcomers. This gave him the opportunity to move backward a little apart from the crowd and contact his ship. Within minutes he had been beamed back aboard and a plan was forming in his mind. The Romulan vessel would be on the alert against any intruders after the Terran girl's abortive attempt to blow it up, but security aboard the *Enterprise* might be slightly more lax. Also, the *Enterprise* was a bigger ship, and could be more of a threat to him if any hostilities broke out; the *Talon* would be easier for his vessel to handle.

Fortunately, his chief engineer had the second

bomb all ready for him as ordered. The Klingon captain was able to pick it up and have his crew quickly beam him aboard the Federation vessel.

He materialized in a small corridor that led to one of the scarcely used auxiliary power units. Although like all Klingon officers he had been briefed on the general layout of Federation vessels, he was not as intimately acquainted with the design as he was with that of the Romulans. The latter were almost identical to Klingon cruisers, but this was strange and subtly different.

It took him several minutes to orient himself properly and decide where he wanted to go. Then, with all the stealth of a born sneak-thief, he slinked along his chosen route unseen by any of the *Enterprise's* crew.

When Kirk looked around the arena and saw that the Klingon captain was not there, he knew there was going to be trouble. "Spock, Scotty, get down here on the double," he called. As the two men came out of the stands to join him, Kirk pulled out his communicator and informed the *Enterprise* that there would be three to beam up, almost immediately.

"What about us, Jim?" McCoy asked, indicating the rest of the party from the ship.

Kirk shook his head. "I only need people familiar with the technical workings of the ship. If we can't stop Kolvor, there's little more you could do—and in that event, I'd prefer you were safely down here."

By that time, Spock and Scotty were at the captain's side. Kirk gave the order to the ship and the trio immediately felt the strange tingling sensation of the transporter beam. Seconds later they were standing in the familiar surroundings of the Transporter Room aboard the *Enterprise*. Kirk stepped down off the platform and moved quickly to the intercom built into the wall.

"Captain to Bridge," he said crisply. "Condition Red, repeat, Condition Red. Captain to Security:

Intruder Alert. There is reason to believe we have one or more intruders aboard ship with the purpose of sabotage. Search to be concentrated in the Engineering areas. Each security team is to be accompanied by someone from Engineering so that it can know what signs to look for. Intruder or intruders must be presumed armed and dangerous, so I want all phasers set to kill. We can't take any chances."

That done, Kirk turned to his chief engineer. "Scotty, I want you to draw up the search pattern. You know the ship's workings better than anyone else. List the places you'd go to do the most damage if you had only one bomb and very little time."

Scotty scowled. "Aye, captain. I can think of about a dozen, offhand."

"That's what I was afraid of." Turning next to his first officer, Kirk went on. "Spock, come with me to the Bridge. I want you to tie the computers into the internal sensory system to see whether we can find any traces of someone or something that shouldn't be there. If the computer can pinpoint any areas of danger, it might save the search teams some time."

Out in the halls, lights were flashing, sirens were wailing and people were running past them. It looked like total chaos, but Kirk knew it was an orderly confusion. Each member of the crew had his specific battle station and knew how best to reach it from anywhere on the ship. The captain and his first officer pushed their way through the crowd to the nearest turbolift station and waited for the next available car. Both traveled in silence during the trip, which was quicker than usual—during red alert, the turbolifts worked at peak speed, even if it was a little more uncomfortable for the occupants.

Once back on the Bridge, Kirk felt a little more at home, a little more capable of dealing with any problems that might arise. He was at the nexus of the ship, the focal point of everything that happened. Reports were reaching him continually from the scattered teams as they spread out through the ship in search of Klingon sabotage. Behind him, Spock was working with his usual Vulcan efficiency at the computer terminal, looking for any clue that might indicate the presence of the enemy.

Despite the tension of the situation, despite the danger to the *Enterprise* and its crew, Kirk almost felt relieved at being back here where he belonged. This was a threat he could understand and deal with. It was based firmly in reality—unlike the lunacy of Enowil's madcap planet. At least there were rules here that made sense to sensible people.

"Captain," came Spock's voice from behind him. "I believe I've found something."

After a long string of negative reports, Kirk was willing to leap at anything. He bounded out of his command chair and was at the Vulcan's side in a matter of seconds. "What is it?"

"There seems to be a break in the relay override circuits. Take a look for yourself."

Kirk glanced at the schematic drawing on display in Spock's viewer. The relay override circuits were the ship's failsafe mechanism that would inform Engineering instantly of any breakdowns in crucial functions, and would automatically reroute those functions to the backup systems. A ship as big and complex as the *Enterprise* had many backups built into it; a potential saboteur would want to ensure that those secondary systems were out of commission before tackling his main objective. Otherwise, his plans might well go for naught even if he succeeded in planting his bomb.

Kirk was immediately on the intercom to his chief engineer, who was coordinating the search. "Scotty, there's been some damage to System EC-1052. What exactly does that mean?"

There was silence for a moment as the engineer considered the problem. "EC-1052 is the alarm to let us know when something is wrong with the engine coolant system. If it isn't workin', there's no way to switch on the auxiliary coolers."

The situation immediately became obvious to Kirk. The ship's engines generated intense amounts of heat, which had to be constantly drained off by the coolant system. If the refrigeration broke down, the engines would quickly heat up to a critical point and explode, taking most, if not all, of the ship with them. EC-1052 was supposed to prevent that from happening by switching to a backup cooling system in the event of the primary's failure. But if EC-1052 were not working, there could be no switchover, and damage to the main coolant system could mean the destruction of the *Enterprise* shortly thereafter.

"Which teams are checking the coolant lines?" Kirk asked.

"None, Captain. We were checkin' the engines themselves, primarily. Until this minute we didna think a bomb there would be so fatal. I could redirect. . . ."

"Yes, do that, Scotty. I'm on my way there now, myself." Kirk was almost out the door even as he spoke, moving so quickly that even Mr. Spock could not keep up. The turbolift doors had closed behind the captain before the first officer could leave his post and follow. Mr. Spock had to wait another couple of minutes before a second turbolift car arrived to take him, as well, to the area of the ship where the coolant system was based.

For Kirk, the ride was agonizingly long as his car moved first downward and then around in its journey through the ship to the coolant pumps. He took his own phaser out of its holster and checked to make sure it was set to kill. That done, there was nothing for him to do but stand and wait, watching the glowing lights zip by to indicate the turbolift stations he had passed. At any instant he expected to feel the explosion of the Klingon bomb while he was stuck helplessly in this tiny compartment—and yet the seconds ticked relentlessly by and nothing happened.

The car at last came to a jarring halt and the doors swished open in front of him. Kirk raced out into the hallway, phaser drawn and ready for anything. This area of the ship was deserted; under red alert conditions it was not normally manned, as there were more crucial areas requiring attention. Kirk had to run more than thirty meters down this corridor to the crossing branch that would take him to the main coolant pump room, where the saboteur would most likely be.

He was breathless by the time he reached the pump room, and he found the doors locked—from the inside. Impatiently he aimed his phaser at the doors and fired. There was the familiar high-pitched keening, and the doors glowed for a moment before vanishing from the universe. Kirk rushed inside the room, prepared for anything.

Captain Kolvor was there, standing beside a large box he had strapped to the side of one of the pumps. He had been in the process of making final adjustments on it when he'd heard Kirk fire at the door. He was now in the act of turning and pulling his own weapon from its holster as Kirk entered the room and dived for cover.

Kirk fired his phaser the instant he saw the Klingon captain turning toward him. But this time, nothing happened—no sound, no ray . . . nothing. Kirk hit the floor, rolled, and came up in a kneeling position, prepared to shoot again—and again, nothing happened. Kirk looked down with disgust at the phaser in his hand. It had worked a moment ago on the door, so its power pack could hardly be used up. Why was it not working? Why had it betrayed him?

The failure of Kirk's weapon had given Kolvor time to draw his own in defense—but he discovered that it, too, was not working. With a snarl of rage he tossed it aside and began to run back through the doorway from which Kirk had just entered.

Phaser or no phaser, the Federation captain was not about to let Kolvor escape. Getting quickly off his knees, he launched himself in a low dive, tackling the Klingon about the ankles just before he could reach the doorway. The two men sprawled hard onto the ground and began fighting. Kolvor tried to kick his assailant in the face to make him release his hold, but Kirk was able to jerk his neck back to avoid the blow. Instead, he used the Klingon's body as a ladder to pull himself along to a more direct confrontation. He landed a few punches himself to the other's midsection, dodged a blow to his head and managed to connect a solid right to Kolvor's jaw. The Klingon's body went limp, just as Spock and a security team came racing into the room from the outer hallway.

Kirk stood up and hauled Kolvor to his feet. The Klingon captain was still conscious, but in no condition for further fighting; the security detail took him into custody without a struggle.

"You're too late, Kirk," Kolvor gasped breathlessly as the security guards held him. "The bomb's already been set."

Spock, who had gone directly to the bomb while the captain was handing over his captive to the guards, nodded. "He appears to be speaking the truth, Captain. These controls have been adjusted to detonate in less than four minutes."

As out of breath as he was, Kirk knew that his job of preserving the ship was not yet done. He ran back to where his first officer was standing beside the bomb and, with fingers that felt as though they were made of lead, he fumbled at the straps that held the heavy box to the side of the pump. "Tell Scotty to have the Transporter Room standing by," he said as he worked. "We'll have to try beaming this bomb out into space before it can go off."

He finally detached the bomb from its mooring and ran out the door with it, waving aside the guards who moved to help him. *This is my responsibility*, he thought. *If I can't make it to the Transporter Room in time, maybe at least I'll be the only one killed.*

He moved down the long hallway once more to the turbolift station. With each meter he traveled, the bomb seemed to grow heavier in his hands, until he could barely manage to carry it. He announced his destination and the turbolift car took off obediently, speeding through the ship on its desperate mission.

Kirk had to stand there, straining to hold the heavy box, as the seconds ticked relentlessly away. Now there were less than two minutes remaining before the bomb exploded—and it seemed to his heightened senses as though the turbolift car were not moving at all.

After eons of agony, the doors slid open once more and Kirk emerged from the turbolift. Fortunately he did not have as long to walk this time; the Transporter Room was just across the hall, only a few meters away from the station.

He staggered into the Transporter Room and found that Scotty was all ready for him. The engineer's hands lifted the bulky box away from him and set it gingerly on the transporter platform. Then Scotty crossed the room and took up his station at the controls. By shifting the lever forward, the transporter hummed to life. The bomb shimmered in the air for a moment, then disappeared.

Kirk breathed a sigh of relief as he leaned back against one bulkhead. The immediate threat to the *Enterprise* was over. "Where did you send it, Scotty?" he asked.

"Just out into space, Captain. With so little time, I didna want to fiddle with fine tunin'."

Kirk nodded slowly. As soon as his legs felt strong enough to walk again, he staggered across the room to the intercom. "Kirk to Bridge. Keep an eye on the monitors. I want to know exactly how potent that bomb was."

A few moments later, the answer came back from a very shaky-voiced lieutenant. "Sir, there was no explosion . . . exactly. The bomb simply disappeared from our monitors, and in its place were the large, glowing letters: B-O-O-M."

Kirk closed his eyes in frustration. *Dame that Enowil and his obscene sense of humor!* he thought.

When he opened his eyes again, he was no longer aboard the *Enterprise*.

For the entrance...

17

He had been transported back to the arena where he and the others had been when Metika and the Romulan appeared. Beside Kirk, looking slightly dazed, were Scotty, Spock and Captain Kolvor. Enowil waited for them down in the center of the arena, along with the rest of the parties that had stayed behind while this current adventure had occurred.

Kirk stalked up to the eccentric Organian and wagged an accusing finger at him. "You caused my phaser to misfire up there, didn't you?"

"Of course, Captain," Enowil said pleasantly. "I also made Kolvor's gun misfire. You're all my guests here; it would be impolite for me to let you kill one another."

"Whether you allowed it or not, Kolvor certainly tried hard enough to hurt people," Commander Probicol said. "I demand to know what you intend to do about it."

"Ah, justice is truth in action," said the gnome. "Captain Kolvor, you certainly have behaved in a most unbecoming fashion, and I hardly think you deserve to play any further part in our festivities. Begone, sir, and take your ship with you."

The Klingon captain opened his mouth to protest,

but before any sound could be uttered he had totally vanished from the arena. Gone, too, were the other members of the Klingon contingent. Kirk suspected that, were he to call up to the *Enterprise*, he would find that the entire Klingon vessel had vanished from Enowil's bubble of nonreality. The contest had now become one between the Federation and the Romulans—but Probicol was certainly threatening to make it a heated confrontation.

"What about them?" he continued, waving a hand to indicate Kirk's group. "They also tried to sabotage me."

"Accuse not Nature, she hath done her part; do thou but thine," Enowil scolded him. "Captain Kirk's protestations of innocence are correct—he knew nothing of the woman's actions. And she herself merely acted at the instigation of Captain Kolvor. I shan't take any action against her, though the two of you may wish to settle the matter between yourselves."

"I'll teach her how the Romulans deal with saboteurs," Probicol growled.

"Not so fast," Kirk said. "She's still a passenger from my ship, under my jurisdiction. By attempting to disrupt relations between your Empire and ourselves, she's violated a number of our own laws, and she's in very serious trouble." He glared at Metika to let her know he meant what he said. "I can assure you, Commander, she will be severely punished for what she has done."

The Romulan commander gave a small snort, but said nothing.

Metika turned to look at Probicol. "What . . . what will happen to Lieutenant Breccio?" she asked tentatively.

Commander Probicol drew himself up stiffly. "That need not concern *you*. He lied to me about your part in this affair, which is a breach of his duty. Whatever misguided reasons he had for doing so, he will learn better for the next time—if, indeed, there is a next time."

While this interchange had been going on, Dr. McCoy came up to Kirk and tapped him on the shoulder. "Jim, could I speak to you privately for a moment?"

"What about, Bones?"

"Well, after you returned to the ship, nothing much happened here. Enowil disappeared, and I figured he was probably going to watch you. I figured he must really enjoy watching us jump through our paces for him—and that set me thinking about some other things. . . ." He and Kirk moved away from the main group, and lowered their voices so no one else could hear them.

Metika took this opportunity to look over at Breccio. The young Romulan was standing at rigid attention, even though his commander had moved away and was momentarily ignoring him. "That was a very noble thing you did," Metika said softly. "Telling your commander lies to try to save me."

"It wasn't noble," Breccio said. "It was stupid."

"Then why did you do it?"

Although he remained at attention, there seemed to be a slight movement of uncertainty in his body. "I don't know," he said, and he deliberately did not look at her as he spoke.

"Our agreement was up," Metika persisted. "You didn't have to protect me."

"I am aware of that."

"Could it be that you started thinking about me as a person instead of as an enemy?"

Breccio did not reply immediately, and he was saved from having to answer at all by the return of Captain Kirk. The commander of the *Enterprise* was looking at Enowil with a confident grin illuminating his features.

"I think we've solved your riddle," Kirk told the gnome. "It should have been obvious from the very fact that you brought us here in the first place. Your behavior in showing us around has only made it clearer."

"Now you're the one speaking in riddles, Captain," Enowil said, intrigued. "Please let me know what your idea is."

"Do you remember how disappointed you were when I didn't want to see the rest of the zoo? And how disappointed when Lieutenant Uhura didn't like the lion you made for her? And how disappointed when we didn't want to watch the rest of the 'adventure' you planned? You wanted us to enjoy those things as much as you did, and you were downcast when we didn't. What you need, Enowil, is an audience."

The Organian looked at Kirk for a moment and wrinkled his brow. "You mean like this?"

The stands of the arena around them were suddenly full of people. Some were cheering madly, some were laughing, others gasping in horror. The roar of the crowd was almost deafening.

Kirk closed his eyes and shook his head slowly. "No, not at all. You've already proved you can create people. You can make people who are happy, sad, brave or cowardly. You can make people who can agree or disagree with you. But, by the very nature of your powers, you can't create someone who exists independently of you, who has a judgment of his own that functions without reference to yours. That's what you need.

"You brought us here to show off what you could do. Indirectly, you've been asking our opinions of everything you create. When we admire something, you're happy; when we don't, you're depressed. You brought us here to be critics, to be your audience— because that's what you really need. We're not paid to laugh at your jokes, or even to argue with you. You don't know how we'll react, and that's what sets us apart from your creations. You want to please us because our independent opinions are the ones that matter."

Enowil was uncharacteristically silent for a long moment. Then suddenly he began to whirl like a top, faster and faster until all his features were blurred and ran together. He started to fade, until after a few seconds there was nothing there at all.

"I hope he doesn't get mad, Jim," McCoy said softly. "Remember the story of Rumplestiltskin."

But the doctor's worries were for naught. Enowil reappeared almost immediately, looking as bright and chipper as ever. "You are absolutely right, Captain. Brilliant. Every creator must have someone to create *for*—and I, as one of the greatest creators, need an equally great audience. I shall have to give some thought to acquiring one from somewhere.

"In the meantime, Captain, I am in your debt. As I promised, the reward goes to you. Name your heart's desire, and it will be yours."

Kirk looked over at Commander Probicol. The Romulan leader was clearly worried about what Kirk might choose, though he tried hard to look unperturbed. Kirk toyed with the idea of letting him suffer for a while, then decided that would be needlessly cruel. "Actually," he said to Enowil, "I think we can work out the favors to our mutual advantage."

Predictably, the Organian looked curious. "In what way, Captain?"

"When you snatched us out of our universe and brought us here, we were on a mission of mercy. There was a colony world that was proving unsuitable for the people living there; their very lives could be in peril unless we evacuate them and take them . . . somewhere. The thought occurred to me that perhaps you could . . ."

"Bring them here!" Enowil completed the thought enthusiastically. "Of course. Nothing could be simpler."

Kirk shifted his weight slightly. "I wasn't thinking

of here, precisely. These are ordinary people, remember; they might not be able to stand a constant diet of . . . um, the more *unusual* aspects of your world. What I was thinking was that you could create another planet for them, one that obeys the ordinary laws of physics, where they could live in peace. Then, for holidays and special occasions, they could come here and view your creations."

"The ordinary laws of physics—how tedious," Enowil said. "Still, you did solve my problem; you have but to ask and it shall be done." His face brightened suddenly. "Perhaps it's best that they do have such a humdrum planet; then they'll be able to appreciate my creations even more."

"Of course," Kirk said, anxious to encourage Enowil along that line of thought. "If everything around them were so strange, they'd begin taking it for granted. Oh, and while you're transporting them to their new world could you make the people healthy at the same time? Could you eliminate all traces of argon poisoning in their systems?"

"No problem at all. I shall be delighted to do whatever I can for these people. I'll give them the best planet this universe—or any other—has ever seen. They'll have everything they could ever want."

"Including freedom?" Kirk asked. "They must have freedom to travel out of this bubble, to and from the rest of the Federation, to communicate back and forth—and above all, they must have the freedom to leave if they choose. A good critic must always reserve the right to walk out if the performance is too bad."

"You drive a hard bargain, Captain Kirk," Enowil said. "But a fair one. Their freedom will be as precious to me as my own. I see I didn't misjudge you—you are a wise and a just man."

"Thank you." Kirk started to turn away, then stopped. "One more detail. This new planet should be named Spyroukis—in honor of the Federation's most distinguished explorer."

Enowil nodded, and Kirk turned to Metika. "Does this meet with your approval?"

There were tears of joy brimming over in the girl's eyes. "Oh, Captain, I couldn't have dreamed for better."

Enowil cleared his throat. "If I may be permitted a minor suggestion, Captain?"

"What is it?"

"These two young people—" He indicated Metika and Breccio. "They're both in serious trouble if they go back to their respective worlds. Here, they too would be free. Why don't we have them stay and become the first citizens of our new world?"

"I have no objections," Kirk smiled, glancing at Metika one more time.

"Well, I do," Commander Probicol said. "This is an outrage. You are tampering with the Romulan system of justice, and you have no right to do so. Lieutenant Breccio will return with his ship and face the charges against him like a Romulan."

"I should think, sir, that the choice was up to the lieutenant." Enowil's voice was very soft, but there was no mistaking the quality of command in it. When he chose, the Organian could be quite forceful.

All eyes went to Breccio. The young Romulan was almost paralyzed with indecision. He had been brought up according to the strict Romulan code of personal honor and duty. He had broken that code already by lying to his superior; by all rights he should pay the penalty for his dishonor. If he were to take the coward's way out by staying here, his name and his family would be disgraced. Feelings of guilt and shame were rising strongly to the front of his mind. He stood there in the arena, shaking and perspiring, while everyone stared.

Without taking her eyes from his face, Metika Spyroukis raised her arms outward toward him. "Marcus Claudius Breccio, please stay here with me. I would be honored."

Breccio turned his head to look at her closely for perhaps the first time. She was beautiful, he thought —in a human sort of way. What was more important, she wanted him. She said she would be honored to have him stay with her. He realized that it was better to stay where one was honored than to go where one was not. Perhaps his family and his name would be disgraced by his desertion; but weren't they already disgraced by his lying and his treason in abetting an enemy? One more disgrace could hardly matter.

"I'll stay," he said quietly.

Commander Probicol was furious. He took a step toward Breccio, perhaps with violence in mind, but nothing ever came of it. Enowil had merely to raise his hand, and the Romulan leader—together with his entire contingent except for Breccio—vanished from the arena.

"They are aboard their ship again, back in their home territory," Enowil said simply. "I trust that will mollify them a little."

Breccio and Metika walked toward each other, arms outstretched as though in a dream. Their hands locked, and they stood staring into one another's eyes as though the rest of the people in the arena did not exist. Taking their cue, Enowil and the Federation party walked away to leave the two young people alone for a while.

"It may take me a few days to create the new planet, Captain," Enowil admitted. "A whole new world takes time to make."

"Legend has it that you need six days," Dr. McCoy said.

"Bah. Only for the unskilled or the unpracticed. I'll only need three at the most. In the meantime, Captain, I'll let you return to your ship, with my thanks."

"I have to thank you too, for helping solve our problem," Kirk smiled. "And for providing us with a very *entertaining* experience."

"The little foolery that wise men have makes a great show," Enowil said, then winked. "Farewell, Captain."

Kirk and the rest of his crew found themselves suddenly back aboard the *Enterprise*, standing on the Bridge. The viewscreen at the front showed not the milky luminescence of Enowil's bubble, but the blackness of space dotted by the diamond dust of stars. They were back in their own familiar universe once more, in orbit around Epsilon Delta 4.

Dr. McCoy moved up to stand at the captain's elbow. "I think you made the right decision about the wish, Jim. But all the same, don't you suppose you'll wake up sometimes in the middle of the night and wonder what else you might have wished for?"

The same thought had occurred to Kirk. "Anything our hearts desired. With a whole universe to choose from, what couldn't we have had? Wealth, women, power, immortality—the human soul can be a greedy beast. It's a frightening thought, Bones. That's why I made the choice quickly, before I had the chance to think of something selfish."

He looked over at his first officer. "But I wonder—what would you have asked for, Mr. Spock, if the choice were up to you?"

"That's nonsense, Jim," Dr. McCoy said. "Everyone knows Vulcans have no wishes or desires."

"On the contrary, Doctor," Spock said calmly. "I could always have wished for a little less sarcasm from those around me."

And for once, McCoy was at a loss for words.

FINIS

ABOUT THE AUTHOR

STEPHEN GOLDIN is a young science fiction writer who lives with his wife, Kathleen Sky, in California. He has several other science fiction titles to his credit.

THE EXCITING REALM OF STAR TREK

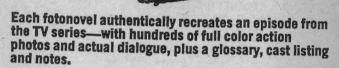